From the files of the Free City Inquisitor's Office:

I0654151

Torn From On High
Free City Book 2

S F Chapman

striped
cat
Press
www.stripedcatpress.com

Torn From On High
Free City Book 2
by
S F Chapman
is also available
as a Kindle e-Book

Learn more about the author at www.SFChapman.com

The phrases "From the files of the Free City
Inquisitor's Office," "The Free City Series,"
"The MAC Series"
and
the pawing cat logo are trademarks of
Striped Cat Press.

Visit us at www.stripedcatpress.com

Cover by Mae Yamo

Copyright © 2014 S F Chapman
All rights reserved.
ISBN-10: 0985536993
ISBN-13: 978-0-9855369-9-2

Striped Cat Press
First Paperback Edition, First Printing:
May 2014

P1e1pb4

To Mark,
the best of all brothers

Acknowledgements

Producing a novel is a cooperative endeavor. The author struggles with the words and story for many months in the quest to create a manuscript but it is the editors who really make the work into a novel that can be enjoyed by nearly everyone.

I would like to thank my three longtime editors for their efforts in helping me to craft *Torn From On High* into the exciting book that you hold in your hands. Christina, Mark and Clint spent many hours reading, marking up and discussing the early manuscripts with me and I believe that it is a better book because of their hard work.

Thank you all.

Introduction

If by chance you have not yet read *The Ripple in Space-Time* which is the first book in the Free City Series, may I suggest that doing so will greatly increase your understanding of the characters in the series and the gritty post-apocalyptic world of 2446.

It is a dark and gritty Film Noir-like world with danger and scoundrels skulking around every corner. Nearly all humans on Earth and beyond live in subjugation as serfs or slaves under the domination of a few corrupt Warlords.

The exception is the small autonomous zone of Free City at the northern end of the Shannon River valley in what was once known as the Republic of Ireland. Free City could easily be mistaken for twenty-first century London, San Francisco or Manhattan. Although it has the typical ills of all metropolitan areas, Free City is the sole bastion of Law, scientific research and progressive thinking. By long standing agreement with the Warlord Syndicate, the Free City High Court tends to all judicial matters. The Registry Bureau regulates motor vehicles, boats and ships, aircraft and spacecraft. The Free City Inquisitor's Office, a future version of Scotland Yard or the FBI, is often called in to investigate difficult crimes wherever they occur.

The Free City Series follows many of the cases that Inspector Second Class Ryo Trop, the Inquisitor's Office's most talented cop, has undertaken.

As a counterpoint to the action, I have included several News Items from 2446. These short articles are often written in what would now be called a sensationalized tabloid style with the heavy-handled use of adverbs and adjectives. The News Items sometimes provide subtle clues for readers who like to "solve" the crime before the protagonist does.

A list of the characters along with brief personal histories has been provided in the Appendix.

Please enjoy *Torn From On High*

1. *Dreg's Scamp*

"There it friggin' is!" Nate Briggs scowled.

Far below him was the derelict hulk that he'd been sent out to recover.

Clad in an ancient and ill-fitting spacesuit, he dangled precariously upside down at around a hundred and twenty kilometers above the northwestern Pacific in the open cockpit of the beat-up little salvage runabout that long ago had been scornfully dubbed *Dreg's Scamp*.

At the ragged and turbulent boundary between the thin outer atmosphere of the Earth and space, buffeted relentlessly by ionized oxygen atoms, the house-sized object glowed with a faint pinkish hue.

At least a dozen times a day for many years, Captain Takahashi had dispatched Nate from the mother ship, now thirty kilometers higher up in a much safer orbit, to wrangle and retrieve marginally valuable space debris before it plunged into the thicker atmosphere below and burned up.

The Captain had made millions over the years in the risky business of space junk recovery; Nate, of course, had made nothing. Serfs were rarely paid.

1

Torn From On High

"Come on, Nate! I don't friggin' have all day," the Captain harangued him over the radio. "Pick up the pace. Time is money!"

"Yes sir, I'm working on it," Nate meekly replied.

This particular bit of scrap metal, which Nate guessed was probably a three hundred year-old rocket booster from the late 21st century, was going to be an especially difficult snatch. "I won't be able to use the dragline, I don't see anything that the hook could snag."

"Use the bridle, you moron!"

Nate winced; the bridle was a huge, cup-shaped steel net that could be tugged behind the little salvage craft by long cables. It worked quite well when recovering large, well-behaved objects in much higher orbits, but at the fringe of the atmosphere the giant net might catch the thermosphere and act like a braking parachute. He and the rickety runabout would be pulled inexorably downward to a fiery demise.

"Alright;" Nate sighed, "I'm deploying the bridle."

He pulled himself out of the tight cockpit, stood cautiously on the open deck of the runabout and cast off the heavy net. The bridle wafted and fluttered slightly as it unfurled. With his safety cable firmly clamped to the railing, Nate straightened up to watch the progress of the drifting net.

"What the hell?" At the far edge of his peripheral vision, a curious pulsing purple glow caught his attention.

Nate cringed in agony.

Several vertebrate in his neck briefly sizzled and sputtered under the narrow intense beam of high-energy neutrons before they shattered and severed his spinal cord.

He was paralyzed!

The spacesuit air leak alarm squealed and the self-sealing membrane slowly contracted.

Nate cursed to himself.

He'd been saved from a quick and merciful death by the automatic safety system only to undoubtedly suffer a much more gruesome fate.

He could barely breathe and certainly couldn't speak.

"NATE! Get it friggin' together and haul that crap back up here!" The Captain was obviously unaware of his predicament.

The falling bridle caught the edge of the booster and the cables drew taut. The added drag and mass of the net jerked the rocket and the trailing runabout downward. Nate was flung limply from the little vessel. Still tethered to the *Scamp* by the safety line, he bobbed face down like a buoy in rough seas.

Below him, the jumble of ensnared debris was rapidly falling out of orbit.

He watched impassively for several minutes as he was dragged steadily towards the cloud-dappled ocean below.

Nate lost consciousness just as the outer layer of the spacesuit burned away in the angry and abrasive atmosphere.

Two minutes later, he was dead.

2. The Connaught School for Disadvantaged Girls

The adorable little group of a half-dozen six and seven-year-old violinists were nervously preparing on the high auditorium stage.

Two dour instructors pointed and nodded sternly to each of the girls as they took their places and tuned up their ancient violins.

Tentative squawks and screeches emanated from the finicky instruments.

Seated nine rows back in the crowded venue, Ryo smiled at the protracted preparations; the set up alone would likely take longer than the allotted seven minute portion of the show by the aspiring young recitalists.

With the tap of a long thin baton, the group began with a scratchy rendition of *Mary Had A Little Lamb*.

They were surprisingly good for first year music students at The Connaught School for Disadvantaged Girls, Ryo realized.

He had come to the early evening Mid-Summer Recital not for the sextet of former ragamuffins-turned-string virtuosos but for one particular twelve-year-old girl who would perform at the end of the show.

Fifty-six year-old ex-Investigator for the Free City Inquisitor's Office recently turned Government Granted Guardian of a Minor, Ryo Trop, had come to watch his charge, Dilma, at her first big public event. She was now a lovely and cheery young lady, Ryo mused, but nearly a year ago she'd been a downcast and enslaved parlormaid for the recently assassinated Warlord of the Outer Reaches.

Dilma had provided invaluable aid to a group of three spies that had eventually dispatched the despised Warlord and they had returned the favor by rescuing her from the palace on Saturn's moon Titan.

A mutual friend had introduced her to him four months later at the Low Earth Orbit Acclimatization Station. Dilma urgently required an especially steady hand to guide her into adulthood and Ryo needed a suitably compelling justification to nudge him into early retirement.

For two weeks the former slave girl and the soon-to-be retired Investigator got to know each other as they ran on treadmills and worked out on exercise machines to strengthen themselves for the rigors of terrestrial gravity.

Ryo spent hours at the large portholes of the space station patiently identifying the ever-changing features for her on the Earth below.

Dilma was fascinated by the size and stark detail of the planet. She had heard astonishing assertions about the beauty of the home world of humanity during her eleven years on Titan but had never conceived of personally substantiating the claims.

Ryo smiled as he recalled that early on she had pointed in awe to the wide and irregular sections of blue that adorned the surface. He explained that vast amounts of liquid water covered much of the Earth. The refugee from the icy Saturnian moon spent hours afterwards asking him progressively more complex questions about the oceans.

At "night" she would sleep nuzzled next to him as they floated about in his tiny cabin. She was a fidgety and turbulent bedmate. He had often lain awake and considered the nearly crushing adversities that she had thus far endured. With disconcerting regularity Dilma suffered through horrifying nightmares; in the "morning" she would often share them with him after some negligible prompting.

For nearly two weeks, she'd been a ravenous eater. Ryo had mused that in less than a fortnight she was attempting to make up for over a decade of starvation. Finally, near the end of their stay, Dilma tapered off to the normal appetite of a healthy preteen.

On their final day at the space station, the Psychologist met privately with Dilma to ask her if she would be willing to live with Ryo in his cramped apartment in Free City. The doctor reported that she stared at him in amazement before answering; she had never been given a choice of any consequence in the past, "Of course;" she'd whispered, "Who else would I live with?"

The tiny violinists finished up their final song and stood proudly to receive the hardy applause. After several ungraceful and uncoordinated group bows, the little girls filed off the stage.

During the doldrums between acts, many members of the audience quietly rearranged themselves.

Ryo felt a tap on his shoulder.

It was Dr. Jana Fesai, his companion of late and perhaps, he hoped, eventually his sweetheart. Ryo and his colleagues had freed the brilliant fifty-three year-old Physicist last year from the space pirates who had kidnapped her. The two had slowly become good friends on the long trip back to Earth.

"Hi," she whispered.

Ryo shuffled over one seat and Jana sat next to him.

"I'm glad that you could make it."

The show began anew with a short skit by several eight and nine year-olds.

Her hand wandered over to his and Ryo clasped it in smug victory.

She had returned to Free City after her abduction and taken up the long-vacant Research Director position in the Department of Ultra Energy Physics at Free City University. The occupation was maddeningly time consuming, which had led to an unforeseen side effect; they both cherished the brief and scattered intervals that they spent together.

The skit ended and the players left the stage to be replaced by a quartet of guitar-wielding ten year-olds.

Ryo spotted Dilma waiting nervously in the wings; she would be the next to perform.

A few weeks after they'd left the space station for Earth, Ryo enrolled his young charge in the acclaimed Connaught School for Disadvantaged Girls in the Ballaghaderreen District of Free City.

Torn From On High

A day or two after she'd begun her studies, Ryo ventured back to the Inquisitor's Office at City Hall with the full intent of asking for his early retirement. After more than thirty-five years of hard work as an Investigator, he reasoned, he certainly deserved an early release. Dilma would surely require nearly constant oversight for years to come.

His perpetually sour seventy year-old boss, Chief Inspector Helga Bennet, thought otherwise.

The Inquisitor's Office could not risk permanently losing its best Investigator, she sternly told him, particularly not during the current state of unprecedented upheaval in the city and beyond.

The two old friends doggedly debated the issue for hours.

Finally a compromise was reached that satisfied neither of them: Ryo would be immediately promoted to the nearly unheard of rank of Inspector First Class, second only to Helga's standing as Chief Inspector, and be placed on indefinite paid leave. He would return to service only if dire circumstances required it.

In the many months since then, Helga had contacted him only twice with several minor questions regarding past investigations.

At last Dilma journeyed alone across the empty stage. She looked disconcertingly small and timid as she waited for the audience to quiet down.

The spectators gradually fell silent.

"All our yesterdays have lighted fools the way to dusty death!" she thundered. "Out, out, brief candle!"

Jana squeezed Ryo's hand in excitement at the girl's choice of material; the woman had been an avid reader of Shakespeare for most of her life and undoubtedly knew the speech from *Macbeth* well.

"Life's but a walking shadow; a poor player, that struts and frets his hour upon the stage," Dilma continued.

Ryo glanced sideways; Jana was silently mouthing the lines along with the girl.

"And then is heard no more: it is a tale told by an idiot, full of sound and fury," she paused dramatically and held her hands high, "SIGNIFYING NOTHING!"

The audience roared for the passionate young thespian.

Dilma continued with a speech from *Romeo and Juliet* and *As You Like It* before she bowed proudly and swaggered off the stage.

The recital ended and the audience stood to leave the venue.

Jana kissed Ryo's cheek, "I've got to get back to the lab, dear. We're right in the middle of a finicky ultra energy particle collision study."

The old investigator smiled at his incessantly busy friend.

"Oh; I almost forgot," Jana handed him a rumpled copy of the Recital program, "Professor Evans asked me to give you this note."

"Malcolm Evans from the School of Biology?" he stared at her in surprise.

She nodded, "He *was* in the back row; although I don't see him there now."

Ryo swiveled around and tried in vain to spot the elusive middle-aged Professor.

Jana slipped on her overcoat and shrugged, "I guess he had to get back to the University as well, but he did mutter something about wanting to see a parlormaid perform. Whatever that means."

"Who knows," he frowned.

Ryo watched her hurry off towards the exit.

When Jana disappeared into the throng of fashionably attired attendees, he glanced down to study Malcolm's note.

In overly large and scrawly black handwriting it simply read:

Contact Zmuda As Soon As Possible.

3. Transits

Halfway through their slow and unfortunately unescorted tour of the University's Ultra Energy Lab, the wide-eyed preteen stopped to handle some lab equipment left unattended on a workbench.

"What's this thingy?" Dilma held up the oddly shaped metal widget.

Ryo studied the strange curvy object for several seconds before shrugging, "I have no idea. You can ask Dr. Fesai when she not too busy."

Dilma glanced back towards Jana's office where the overworked scientist was shuffling through a tall stack of paperwork.

Ryo noticed that the youngster had her all too common look of curiosity and annoyance as she returned the implement to the table. He had seen the expression enough recently to know that the former slave girl craved to learn of every tiny detail about the fascinating world in which she now lived and was exasperated when she could not gain the precious knowledge immediately.

An hour ago they had stopped by the lab to take Jana up on her standing offer of a tour. But a frantic grad student had waylaid the woman with some anomalous results in a massive particle collision study that threatened to disrupt the ongoing experiment. Jana had profusely apologized to Dilma before retreating to her office to deal with the minor catastrophe.

Now the old investigator found that he was unwittingly leading the inquisitive little girl through the lab.

She stared up at him with dark, saucer-shaped eyes. "What shall we look at next, Daddy?"

Ryo smiled at the girl, "There's a small particle accelerator in the basement that we can peek at, I have no idea of how it works but it has plenty of pipes and wires."

"OK," Dilma pouted a bit at the prospect of seeing more great things without receiving sufficient explanations.

Ryo pointed to a door and they shuffled off.

The old Investigator sighed as they walked down the hallway together; he had to get some help for the formidable task of raising the girl.

• • •

It was about 3 AM, she groggily estimated.

The tiny apartment that they shared was uncomfortably cold, Keira realized as she snuggled closer to Lev in a sleepy attempt to purloin some of his body heat.

The chilliness of the last several days matched her mood.

After months of relative peace between the two of them, Lev had gotten restless again and decided to take a break from his efforts to complete his doctorate studies at the University.

The relentless tug of the Enlightenment Crusade seemed to be pulling him away from her.

Keira dreaded his involvement with the mildly subversive student group not only because it drew his attention away from their relationship but also because the organization contained a great many attractive and promiscuous women.

Before Ryo Trop had introduced them, Lev had bed-hopped with far too many of the Crusaders. It had taken months of effort on Keira's part to get Lev to settle down and pledge monogamy to her. They had even talked recently of engagement and eventual marriage.

She shivered in the cold apartment.

In the morning, after stopping by to see his mother in the Old Town District, Lev would

16

leave for New Rome with a group of activists to agitate for slave's rights in EurAfrica. Many of the Crusaders had been jailed in New Rome in the last few months and three had even been killed in skirmishes with the locals.

Keira had made him swear that he would exercise caution and remain faithful but she certainly had doubts.

She stroked the profuse hair on his chest as he slept and listened wistfully to the slow cadence of his breathing.

The physical hazards of social activism seemed minor compared to the carnal perils presented by pretty young women.

• • •

Well, that's odd.

Chief Inspector Helga Bennet slowly reread the Daily Unsolved Crimes Briefing in her dim workroom at the Free City Inquisitor's Office.

An unusually high number of suspicious deaths had been recorded in the Space Salvage Industry in the last three weeks.

The curmudgeonly woman thumbed through a stack of reports on her desk for a file that she'd read two days earlier from Mariner's Station on Mars.

Helga scanned the rather routine Crime Scene Report.

The description of Decedent Number 2 listed the poor soul's occupation as "Grappler's Mate" onboard the Salvage Ship *Defiance*.

The recent murder on Mars seemed to fit right into the crime wave.

Why would someone target junkmen? They *were* a rough-and-tumble group but otherwise fairly innocuous.

She would certainly alert the Prime Minister to her suspicions during this morning's daily update.

Undoubtedly the Prime Minister would direct the Inquisitor's Office to investigate further.

The bigger problem, Helga ruminated as she stacked the reports together, was that the inquiry would require an Investigator of the highest expertise.

Unfortunately her best man was currently unavailable.

• • •

They stood together in the little foyer of the townhouse on Breton Street where Jana had raised Lev, he in his traveling clothes and she in her bathrobe and slippers, both dreading the icy harshness of the dawn just beyond the front door.

Jana Fesai briefly glared at her son, "I have to say that I'm rather disappointed that you've decided to put off your studies again."

"*Sorry,*" Lev cringed at the scolding.

Only she was able to induce guilt in him for his occasional misdeeds. Try as she might, certainly Keira couldn't invoke the same sense of shame that his mother could effortlessly produce. "I like to think that I'm helping to improve the lives of others, Mom."

Jana softened a bit as she straightened the wide collar of his chartreuse Pea Coat; "I suppose that *is* a noble cause."

He brushed her fidgety fingers away from his finery, "Thanks; I wish that Keira felt the same way."

"Well;" Jana groaned, "you *are* leaving your rather temperamental fiancée in the lurch to head out to the dangers of New Rome. I can't say that I'm unsympathetic towards the poor sweet thing."

He stared at her in consternation for several seconds, "It's important that I help to free the enslaved and better the lives of the disadvantaged in EurAfrica."

She nodded.

The young man hoisted his knapsack and pulled open the door.

"Be careful;" she caught his arm and reached up to kiss his cheek, "and remember that you're the most important person around for both Keira and I."

"Don't worry Mom;" Lev finally smiled, "I know."

4. News Item: One year on: The destruction of Arusha

Dateline: 2nd of August, 2446; Free City, Earth

In a grim testament to its significance in the recent history of humanity, essentially all members of our lowly species recall where they were one year ago today when they learned of the barbaric destruction of the opulent EurAfrican capital of Arusha.

At the time of the colossal aerial blast high above the Maasai steppes, no one knew of the treacherous and vengeful plot by the now thankfully slain Supreme Imperial Warlord of the Outer Reaches, Dimitri Verhovnyi against his half-brother, Daniel Kufuzu, the Exalted Warlord of EurAfrica.

The petty sibling squabble instigated by Verhovnyi caused the madman to engage several bands of space pirates to fulfill his wicked desire to slay his brother.

The murder weapon was, of course, the huge matter/antimatter explosive device that destroyed the jewel of East Africa.

The most horrific of deeds also massacred nine million residents of the capital city: unfortunate innocents slaughtered by a maniac.

The wide swath of death and devastation had begun exactly two months and one day earlier when Verhovnyi's vile henchmen stole the volatile antimatter used to make the bomb from the Lunar Ultra Energy Research Lab on the plains of the Sea of Crisis, kidnapping several scientists and obliterating the facility to boot.

Amongst those captured by the space raiders was Free City University's most talented researcher, Dr. Jana Fesai. Fortunately, she and most of the other abductees were freed months later by a tenacious and clever band led by Inspector Ryo Trop of the Free City Inquisitor's Office. Most of the exploits that preceded the return of the hostages and the mysterious death of the Warlord of the Outer Reaches remain hidden behind an impenetrable shroud cast over the inquiry by those at the highest levels of Free City Government.

We may never know what really happened in this most horrendous of human affairs.

Those that wish to honor the murdered citizens of Arusha are encouraged to attend memorial services held this evening at the War Atrocities Monument in Roscommon Park.

5. Through the eyes of Sabra MacFarland

She slowly twisted around in the warm, dark room and opened her eyes.

Where was she?

For a good half-minute, twenty-year-old part-time Experimental Studies student Sabra MacFarland tried to silently discover where she had spent the night.

She was sandwiched uncomfortably between two others who were still slumbering. By the particular body odors she guessed that there was a sweaty man to her left and perhaps a recently aroused woman to her right.

Citrus and vanilla? Sabra frowned.

She could barely detect the two fragrances that mingled with the earthy smells of her mysterious bedmates.

Citrus and vanilla were the current favorite variations of incense amongst the loose group of her cohorts in the Enlightenment Crusade.

It was slowly coming back to her now.

Torn From On High

Her pudgy fingers glided lightly over what she guessed was the woman's waist. Fine beadwork on a loosely fitting vest, nothing underneath.

It was probably her older sister Desiree, she decided.

In her thick and over-imbibed state Sabra recalled meeting up with Des and several others at a wild counter-culture club last night.

Screaming Supplicants, Sabra winced.

The club was called *Screaming Supplicants*. There had been strange music and plenty of dancing; certainly stimulants and hallucinogens as well.

Her head throbbed from the recent debauchery.

It would be best if she left before the others awoke. Hopefully no one would remember that she'd been here.

Desiree in particular wouldn't want her cute little sister catching the attention of the warm and sweaty man softly snoring next to her.

She located her clothes and skulked out into a cold adjoining hallway before putting them on.

Sabra tepidly brushed back her grimy brown hair and slipped on her shabby fake fur knee high boots.

Her stomach growled and she was developing a splitting headache.

Sabra tiptoed past several locked doors before she finally found an exit.

Just outside she stood shivering in the chilly early morning gloom on the high front landing of a run down apartment building in one of the seedy outlying districts of Free City.

She still had no idea of where she had ended up.

• • •

After wandering through several nearly deserted blocks, Sabra located a run-down corner bakery that was open.

She smiled hesitantly to the stern and judgmental old man at the counter and ordered a poppy seed bagel and a cup of hot tea.

The skeptical clerk slid the shop's payment interface towards her.

Sabra hoped that she still had some funds in her account to cover the snack.

She swiped her fingertip over the interface.

"*4.25 Standard Units charged to Sabra MacFarland,*" the device replied.

Satisfied with her solvency, the old man twisted around to retrieve a bagel and beverage for her.

The payment interface chirped an unwelcome addition, *"Sabra MacFarland's account balance is now zero."*

The clerk shook his head disapprovingly as he pushed the order towards her.

• • •

It had developed into a particularly crappy morning, Sabra bemoaned as she shivered on the cold bench seat. Fortunately the Free City street transports had always been free, she realized as she bumped along with a few dozing hourly workers in the lumbering old shuttle. Her one essential class at Free City University was in about an hour; hopefully she would be on time.

Sabra felt especially crummy as stared out at the gloominess of the gray early morning metropolis. She hadn't had a bath in weeks, her clothes were tattered and filthy and she was still maddeningly hungry.

In an all too common moment of selfless humanitarianism, Sabra had given away most of her poppy seed bagel to a downtrodden street beggar that she'd met while waiting for the transport to arrive; a noble deed that she now dolefully regretted.

26

• • •

She slipped into the Experimental Studies classroom at Free City University with a few minutes to spare. About a dozen of her scraggily classmates were milling around in the large rectangular room devoid of furniture. *Investigations Into Alternative Lifestyles 501* was an experiential lab class with no need for anything as inhibiting as desks and lecterns. The as-of-yet to arrive instructor had promised that the students would genuinely "feel" their way through the course, both emotionally and physically.

Sabra ruminated on her current lack of funds and her general downward slide towards vagrancy as she regarded her chitchatting peers. Certainly one or two of them would be willing to help out.

She skirted around several of the cattier and well-off teens who had engaged a short high-spirited redheaded woman that Sabra hadn't seen before in the classroom. Sabra sidled up to one of her casual chums; a tall, lanky and often rather conceited fellow named Edlin.

He smirked lasciviously at the possibilities that her arrival might soon produce.

Sabra stroked the profuse hair on his sinewy arm as she cynically trifled with him.

He pressed suggestively against her, "What's up, baby cakes?"

Her eyes twinkled invitingly as she stared up at him, "I ran out of funds this morning. Could you spot me some change for a few days?"

Edlin beamed at his good fortune, his rough hands clasped her waist and crept up towards her breasts.

"What's in it for me?"

A small catlike hand clamped tightly to Edlin's forearm; the long nails, not unlike feline claws, dug into his blotchy flesh. He whimpered from the unexpected assault.

Edlin and Sabra turned in unison towards the assailant.

It was the unfamiliar redhead, now with an especially scornful look of fiery indignation.

"Get lost, you pig!" she growled.

Edlin let loose his hands and left in a huff.

Sabra stared remorsefully at her rescuer, "I know he's a sleazy toss-pot, but I was just trying to borrow a few Units to get me by for a week or so."

28

The mysterious woman softened a bit, "I'll help you out Miss MacFarland, without the need to sell yourself to some greasy low-life for a bit of spare change."

Her savior produced a communication device, "Please credit one hundred Standard Units to Miss Sabra MacFarland."

Sabra studied the visitor with a mix of gratitude and curiosity; her apparently wealthy benefactor had the odd vocal inflections and word choices of a foreigner.

The communications device acknowledged the transaction.

"Thank you so much," Sabra whispered.

As the woman turned to leave the classroom, Sabra caught her arm, "You're new here. Where did you come from?"

The redhead grinned enigmatically, "Long ago from the not-so-wild west, dearie."

She slipped away from Sabra and quickly left the room.

• • •

In the dimly lit anteroom just across the hallway from the classroom now crowded with boisterous

Investigations Into Alternative Lifestyles 501 students, the mysterious visitor studied the screen of her communication device as it connected to that of her colleague in the office.

The face of the middle-aged man appeared, "Zmuda here. What do you have for me?"

The woman grinned mischievously at the question; "I've been trailing her for two days now. You were right Lieutenant; Sabra MacFarland is naive, unkempt and a bit trampy but she has strong ideals and an intriguing underlying sense of street-smarts."

He nodded at the woman's assessment.

"Overall, I think that she's perfect for what you have in mind."

"Good;" he smiled, "we'll make the arrangements right away. Hurry back to headquarters, Sabina."

The connection terminated and the stealthy redhead disappeared into the noisy hallway.

6. 21.080N, 12.271E

Tariq squatted briefly in the shade at the base of the ruins; he set the ancient long-barreled Bedouin rifle against the crumbling old wall and stared across the surrounding dunes.

The sun had risen only about an hour ago and already it was scorchingly hot in the early August desert.

He fidgeted with his shemagh face scarf which was the required orange striped with green wore by all of the Desert Serfs. Although not originally one of the sparsely scattered locals, Tariq was certainly outfitted as one.

The searing heat of the early morning had caused the surrounding sands to simmer hypnotically, he noted.

Their Master at the EurAfrican Imperial Military Base in Tunis had hastily sent Tariq and his two workmates to this desolate inferno a year ago.

After months of sweltering isolation and painstaking work, their vital task was nearing completion.

• • •

For over six and a half thousand years Tunis and its outlying boroughs have suffered through repeated onslaughts.

The particularly strategic coastal promontory with a commanding view of the Gulf of Tunis and the Mediterranean beyond was first settled by Berber traders and later grew to become the fabled Phoenician city of Carthage. The ancient city's location at the southern edge of the narrows between Sicily and North Africa allowed the Carthaginians to tightly control ship traffic and, by extension, trade in much of the eastern Mediterranean.

This advantage quickly led to conflict, most notably with the Romans who eventually enslaved nearly all of the residents after laying waste to the metropolis in 146 BC.

As spiteful as the Romans had been towards the Carthaginians, the location was unmistakably optimal as a trading port and Julius Caesar eventually rebuilt the city. Development quickly spread inland to the area now occupied by Tunis.

When the long Roman rule faltered during the chaos that proceeded the Dark Ages; Genseric, King of the Vandals overtook the city. A half century past before the wobbly remnants of Roman power recaptured the metropolis.

The area later fell to the Arab Muslims that swept across North Africa towards Gibraltar and eventually on into the Iberian Peninsula. Tunis became an important Arab military outpost and trading port during the Dark Ages that shrouded most of Europe to the north in provincial ignorance.

Centuries later during the Eighth Crusade, European Christians briefly tussled with the locals for control of the choice location but the effort proved disastrous. Shortly thereafter Andalusian Muslims and Jews cast out from their homeland arrived in Tunis and the area again flourished in comparative peace for over two hundred and fifty years.

In the 16th Century, the Ottoman Empire battled back and forth with Christians from Spain and Tunis fell for a time into the hands of Europeans. The Ottomans retook the city and it quickly became an opulent center of commerce and skullduggery. Tunis was a primary port for the Barbary Coast pirates that mainly dealt in captured Christian slaves for the Islamic markets of North Africa and the Middle East.

Post-Renaissance Europeans, particularly from France, gradually overtook most of Tunis. The vast French protectorate of Tunisia was established in 1881.

Torn From On High

In 1941 Tunis played an important part in
supplying the legendary Nazi Afrika Korps
under the command of Erwin Rommel in the
North African Campaign of World War II. Men
and munitions were fed in through the port to
carry on the Axis struggle to control the northern
portion of Earth's second largest continent.

Through protracted and agonizing efforts with no
small amount of luck and nearly inexhaustible
resources, the Allied Forces slowly prevailed
over the German-led Axis. The French masters
briefly regained control over Tunisia just after
the war.

But European Colonialism was doomed. One by
one the colonies were set free. Tunisia gained
independence from France in 1956.

Tunisians then enjoyed about two hundred years
of comparative peace before the worldwide
butchery of the protracted Second Amero-Asian
War decimated most human life on Earth.

In a rare bit of luck for the region, by the end of
the Second Amero-Asian War in 2196, Tunis
had been largely spared from the madness that
destroyed the irreplaceable age-old cities of
Cairo, Rome, Athens and many, many others.
Tunis was saved but sadly, most of the residents
were not. For nearly fifty years, great clouds of
radioactive dust and stray plumes produced by
chemical and biological weapons from Northern

Europe drifted south over most of North Africa which denuded the region of nearly all life. By 2300, global warming had caused a 5-meter increase in the water level of the Mediterranean, which cut off the ruins of Carthage from the rest of the sleepy and sparsely inhabited remnants of Tunis.

The abrupt rise of the Warlords in 2363 revived Tunis yet again.

Bwana Kufuzu, the brutal First Warlord of EurAfrica, quickly established a military presence in the region, greatly enhancing his efforts to subjugate the remaining inhabitable portions of Europe to the north. In the ensuing eighty-three years, Tunis has been outshone only by the huge EurAfrican capital of Arusha far to the south as the most populous and wealthy urban area on Earth.

With Arusha's recent destruction, Tunis now ranks as the Earth's most important city.

In an amusing twist of fate, nearly fifty years ago engineers and architects from Tunis were largely responsible for the design and construction of the fledgling city of New Rome. Situated about a hundred kilometers south of the uninhabitable wreckage of the old metropolis, New Rome owes much to its eternally tenacious rival on the Gulf of Tunis.

• • •

Torn From On High

"You will sleep here," the Overseer's Assistant pointed into one of the dozens of doorless rooms in Domestic Servitude Housing Block 43.

The mute slave peered shyly into the austere quarters.

The tattered bed was little more than a narrow cot with a thin gray moth-eaten blanket. A rusty metal washtub and a filthy plastic bucket in the far corner made up the bathroom and laundry facilities.

The shuttered window on the opposite wall contained no glass. The hot afternoon wind from the desert whistled through causing the ill-fitting louvers to rattle disquietingly.

It was above average lodgings for a drudge.

The slave ventured into the chamber that would be his home for the foreseeable future. He set his meager bundle of threadbare clothes on the bed.

"You are permitted one meal per day at the Slave's Dining Hall in Building 3. You are scheduled for 3:25AM until 4:05AM. If you are not present during that time you will not be fed," the Assistant cackled sardonically. "You will report to the Building 17 Slave Master at 6AM tomorrow morning for assignment."

The slave nodded.

• • •

A half an hour further along into his solitary patrol rounds, Tariq stopped for water under an especially desiccated and scraggly palm.

Far to the north, he recalled, in the comparative paradise of Tunis, he and the others had been toiling away on the back-up planning for counterinsurgency should the Fiefdom of EurAfrica face the unlikely prospect of invasion by either IndoPacifica or AmerAsia, its two largest neighbors.

He had been field-testing a crude new handheld particle beam weapon at the Base Ordinance Range when he learned of the news. Nearly a half-day earlier, Outer Reaches hooligans had detonated an antimatter weapon over Arusha and vaporized Daniel Kufuzu, the Benevolent and Exalted Fourth Warlord of EurAfrica.

His Fiefdom was suddenly without the strong and steady hand of a leader, an untenable situation that required immediate and decisive action.

Kufuzu and his advisors had foreseen, although in hindsight imperfectly, just such an unfortunate and despicable event.

The threesome of Paramilitarist Serfs had been sent off from Tunis later that day in a rusty old road machine. Their grueling twenty-one hundred kilometer cross-desert trek had taken nearly a month. Along the way they had acquired, sometimes with cash, sometimes with brutal force, all needed supplies.

Fifteen years earlier their present sweltering location had been selected to be used only if Daniel Kufuzu met with an untimely death.

The long abandoned thousand year-old ruins of the Fort of Djaba and the nearby prehistoric caves lay on the edge of a dune-covered Saharan plateau in the northeastern portion of what had long before been known as the Republic of Niger. The spot had been carefully chosen because of its inhospitable climate and utter isolation.

The idly curious would never stumble upon the forsaken location to interrupt their surreptitious undertaking.

• • •

The mute slave filled the Commander's cup with strong black coffee.

"That will be all," the officer motioned to the door with mild annoyance at the unfamiliar drudge, "now get out."

The slave silently bowed in deference before leaving the office.

Commander of Covert Operations and Feudal Master of Paramilitarist Serfs Frédéric Rameau scowled at the stack of communiqués from Nairobi as he sat stiffly at his desk in the sprawling EurAfrican Imperial Military Base in Tunis.

The ruthless thirty-two year-old former soldier had quickly risen to his current position as Head Spy for the Northern District of Africa when he had thwarted a poorly planned coup six years ago. Daniel Kufuzu himself had personally rewarded Frédéric with the prestigious appointment as thanks for preserving the Warlord's standing as the Supreme Leader of EurAfrica.

But the job had been a letdown for Frédéric. Instead of the intrigue and high drama of fieldwork, he spent nearly all of his time directing two-dozen subordinates from his stuffy little office. Living the vicarious thrills of others was not his style.

He sighed and sipped his now-cold coffee.

Perhaps it wasn't so bad.

His three personal Serfs were hiding out in the desert right now tending to the most vital and unexpected of undertakings. Soon all of humanity would be stunned by what they had managed to accomplish. Certainly as their Master he would personally be credited with achieving the great feat. They were, after all, *just* Serfs.

Frédéric's daydreams of glory were interrupted by the topmost document on the stack in front of him.

He slowly read through the dispatch from an operative in Nairobi.

The man had secretly "befriended" a veteran female Inspector from the Free City Inquisitor's Office and discovered an intriguing bit of information regarding an unsolved crime during a recent drunken dalliance with the woman.

Frédéric reread the message several times and smiled; this, and the work of his Serfs, would change everything.

• • •

With Tariq's return from the patrol of the area adjoining the cave his workmate Qadir trotted out into the heat to replace him on sentry duty.

In the comparative coolness of the well-hidden cave, Tariq bowed reverently to the scruffy man seated comfortably on several burlap sacks of

40

now moldering grain. Grimy, unshaven and dressed as the rest of them were in the malodorous and well-worn garb of the Desert Serfs, the raven-skinned man certainly didn't look like a powerful leader.

He was a bit too dark and delicate in appearance to be successfully passed off as a local, Tariq and his workmates knew, so they had spent days just after they'd recloned him carefully developing a very detailed story that explained the inconsistencies.

The ruse was that the man was a black Arab trader from the island of Lamu a bit south of the equator just off the coast of East Africa. Two years ago, he'd been begrudgingly handed over to a new Master to settle a gambling debt. Now, the elaborate tale went, he tended to group's supplies in the cave because he was too frail for the rigors of the open desert.

"The surrounding area is clear, Oh Exalted One," Tariq held his bow for several seconds.

"Very good, my servant. Shall we begin today's studies?" the man asked.

Tariq nodded, "If it pleases you."

"It certainly doesn't please me, but," he smiled scornfully, "I've come to realize that it is necessary."

Torn From On High

The lightly-built black man rose, "Had my Palace advisors been better prepared for my assassination then I would not have been forced to endure these many months of hiding in the desert whilst I've been reeducated as to what has transpired over the past fifteen years."

Tariq glanced up at the man, "I understand your frustration. Your Aides most certainly failed you by maintaining only out-of-date DNA and memory files. I will strive to keep these vital records current should we be forced by future misfortune to repeat this process."

The Warlord chuckled, "Yes I know. Thank you Tariq; you and your workmates have struggled mightily to rectify the ineptitudes of others."

Tariq relaxed a bit. He was well aware that the recently resurrected EurAfrican Warlord was prone to tirades. It had been long rumored that he had once personally beheaded a hapless Palace slave who had mistakenly delivered the wrong colored grapes to the ruler's breakfast table.

"Tell me," the Warlord began, "how I met my most beloved third wife, Sophia."

7. The cop and the spy

"Inspector Trop," the petite young woman smiled as she stared up at him from behind the desk in the little office, "it is so nice to see you again."

Ryo frowned briefly as struggled to recall when he had last interacted with the ebony beauty. "Ah; Mixion?"

"Right," she twanged with a faint and nearly unidentifiable accent.

"I'm looking for Zmuda."

She grinned pleasantly, "And he is *certainly* looking for you." She produced a communication device, "Jasper, dear; I have a package for the boss."

"On my way," the device replied.

"Which one of his personas is the busiest right now?" Ryo idly asked, "Professor Malcolm Evans of the School of Biology or Lieutenant Zmuda, Master Spy?"

"Definitely Zmuda," Mixion ruminated, "particularly with the current wickedness that is afoot."

Torn From On High

After several seconds of muffled thumps and thuds, the door to what appeared to be a coat closet behind the desk swung open to reveal a husky redheaded man. The garments hung on the closet rod behind him swayed back and forth.

"It's such a remarkably simple way to conceal the entrance to the CRAMP Situation Room," Ryo noted.

The big man loped to the side of the desk.

"We had to enlarge everything last year," Mixion reported, "Jasper was a wee bit too stout to fit through the old passageway."

The redheaded roustabout winced at the ribbing.

Mixion slid open a side drawer of the desk, "Zmuda is in the CRAMP's Bio Lab which is hidden downstairs in the basement of the University's Biology building."

She produced a tattered laminated nametag with a smudged but recognizable image of Ryo and an archaic clipboard with a dozen or so dog-eared documents. "You will need a plausible disguise that will allow you to poke about down there without arousing suspicions."

Ryo studied the badge. *Ned Reed, Vermin Abatement Officer, Free City Health Department* was embossed across the very official looking document.

44

The old Inspector fumbled for several seconds as he attached the nametag to his shirt.

Jasper handed him the clipboard, "Shall we go downstairs for a look-see, *Ned*?"

Mixion rolled her eyes at the minor league deception.

• • •

For twenty minutes Jasper and Ryo kept up the ruse of the stern Heath Inspector and the reluctant University underling scrutinizing the shadowy reaches of the cavernous basement.

When Jasper was satisfied that no one else was lurking about in the sub-level, he casually directed Ryo to a tall and gray electrical panel.

Danger! High Voltage -- Keep Out was boldly painted in bright red letters across the hefty, man-sized cabinet door.

Jasper glanced around before producing a large brass key. With a metallic clank, he unlocked the door and opened it to reveal a second inner panel bestrewn with half a dozen thick black circuit breakers.

The big man deftly toggled several switches.

The inner panel swung open.

Ryo followed him into a dim tunnel and the double doors slowly closed behind them.

After several paces, they stood at a particularly robust metal hatch. A small viewport briefly opened before the massive portal unlatched.

"Ryo Trop! Damn good to see you!" boomed the portly middle-aged gent who greeted them.

"Lieutenant," Ryo bowed slightly to his old cloak-and-dagger friend.

"Welcome to the laboratory."

High up on the back wall in the cheery and well-lit workroom, behind several workbenches cluttered with a bewildering collection of weird metal and glass apparatuses was a carefully lettered sign that proclaimed *Saving humanity: The CRAMP is Combat Ready Advanced Mission Personnel.*

Ryo studied the complex machinery and profuse lab ware; "I must say that you have quite a propensity for setting up large, secret workshops.

Zmuda grinned at the compliment.

"What exactly do you do in here?"

"Mostly hide out from my pesky coworkers," the Lieutenant quipped.

46

Jasper stifled a laugh at the comment.

The spymaster led his guests to several huge shiny metal capsules that stretched from floor to ceiling, all wrapped haphazardly with tangles of tubes and wires.

"This," Zmuda rapped his knuckles against one of the vessels, "is where Jasper was produced."

"Ah; cloning tanks," Ryo nodded. "I myself started out as a baby in a much smaller version of one of these at the EurAfrican Sequential Cloning Facility in Dublin."

The Lieutenant snorted, "You and many thousands of others."

"I think the Dublin facility produced about forty-two hundred infant clones in 2390," Ryo shrugged, "Fortunately only one of me."

"As you may recall, a few years ago I discovered an ancient genetics database from 2060. It of course contained all of the genetic information needed to produce clones, but it also included the memory files of the original adult subjects. Since then I've produced adult clones with all of their memories intact. As far as I can tell, no one else can do anything like this now."

Ryo studied the intricate metal chamber, "It seems that we are still just bumpkins compared to our ancestors in the twenty-first century."

"In many ways, we are. It took months to properly recreate the old process." He pointed proudly at Jasper, "This big lug was the first success."

The Aussie grinned.

"Both Jasper and Mixion recall participating in a secret research project but I've been unable to glean any other information about the effort from the available historical records. It's that old problem that so much information from the past was destroyed during the madness of the Second Amero-Asian War."

Ryo considered the efforts of his friend for several seconds.

Jasper produced a plain, beige photo album and thumbed through several pages, "There are twelve of us now from the distant past, four in Free City and the rest scattered about on Earth and beyond."

Zmuda nodded as the men studied the pictures of the newfangled spies, "We've even got someone on Titan to assure that the recent coup that disposed of the Warlord of the Outer Reaches stays on track."

"Impressive," Ryo commented.

48

The men lingered for several minutes.

"How is Dilma?" Zmuda finally asked with the look of concern that one might expect from a godparent.

"Well enough, I suppose," Ryo dithered as he set the album aside.

"I'm sure that Jana told you that I attended Dilma's recital the other evening as Professor Malcolm Evans. Both Jasper and Mixion were there as well."

Ryo tipped his head and studied the wistful expression on the man's face, "You miss her, don't you?"

Zmuda nodded. "The three of us *did* rescue her from what would likely have been a horrible life in the sex trade."

Jasper had a faraway look as he spoke, "She's such a wonderful young lady. I can't imagine her being abused as an erotic plaything by some brute in the Outer Reaches."

Ryo considered that Dilma had spent months with the three adults during the long return to Earth aboard the tiny interceptor. Certainly the foursome had formed a family of sorts: Zmuda as the wise old patriarch, Mixion and Jasper as the adoring young aunt and uncle, and Dilma as the beloved ragamuffin.

"Just as she was instructed to do," Ryo reported, "Dilma has kept the details of her former life and any reference to you and the CRAMP secret. No one but me knows of her past. But she *does* miss you and sometimes when I'm telling her bedtime stories she will stop me and share a tale about you three."

"She's a great kid," Zmuda beamed.

"And I suspect you're a good dad as well," Jasper added.

"Well," Ryo's eyebrows arched up, "parenting is *so* much harder than investigative work, especially for an elderly novice like me. I have doubts that the fine people at the Connaught School and I can make up for Dilma's frightening lack of social skills and street-smarts."

He sighed as he thought about his cherished young charge, "I'm afraid that she really needs a mother of some sort, or failing that, perhaps a surrogate older sister."

"That has certainly occurred to me as well," Zmuda replied with a catlike grin.

"I would like to return to some occasional investigative work at the Inquisitor's Office."

Ryo studied his old friend with the intuitive eye of a detective, something involving Dilma was lurking about just below the surface, "I'd love to have Jana Fesai take on my little buttercup, but things between us haven't progressed to anywhere near the level that Jana would be comfortable with having someone else's kid calling her mommy."

"Perhaps," Zmuda confessed, "I have a solution for you."

"I thought that you might," Ryo chuckled.

"For a week or so, I've had a new and very stealthy CRAMP agent trail a female student at Free City University that I believe would likely make a good nanny for Dilma."

"Interesting."

Zmuda produced a photo of a rumpled Rubenesque young woman, obviously snapped without her knowledge, "She's scrappy and streetwise but also has a particularly predominant empathy for the downtrodden," he cackled a bit, "and she needs the money."

Ryo studied the image, "She has the long braided hair and the rather revealing clothing of an Enlightenment Crusader."

"Would that be a problem?" Zmuda frowned.

"No; after working with Jana's son last year to track down the missing antimatter, I've grown to greatly admire the efforts of the Crusaders."

"Excellent; we will make the arrangements." Zmuda pointed to Jasper; the big man nodded and silently hurried off.

Ryo watched the burly Australian depart, "I have a feeling that you sought me out for something more than a tour of your secret lab and a sentimental chat about a twelve-year-old."

"Yes;" Zmuda confessed, "those have been amusing little distractions, but not the reason that I need your help."

• • •

Hours later the spymaster concluded his long presentation to the semi-retired cop.

"I don't know how it all fits together yet," Zmuda scowled, "but there is something *very* big and sinister going on somewhere out in the vastness of the North African desert."

"This is spy work," Ryo tapped at the topmost image on the thick stack. "What is my part in all of this?"

"Well;" Zmuda grinned, "about three weeks ago, the Prime Minister signed a secret directive
52

known as Edict 343 which effectively commands all Free City Law Enforcement personal to cooperate unconditionally with the CRAMP in our efforts to destabilize the Warlords, end the repressive feudal system beyond the city limits and bring basic human rights to the masses spread across the Solar System."

Ryo laughed, "Ending servitude, covert insurrection and giving back to the poor? I suppose that makes you something like Abraham Lincoln, Spartacus and Robin Hood in one portly middle-aged package."

"Mmm; don't tell that to Jasper and Mixion, I'll never hear the end of it."

Zmuda continued, "When in doubt while in the company of your colleagues in law enforcement; just smile and say '343.' The effect on those in the know is amazing."

"I'm sure it is." Ryo's eyebrows arched up, "So what is *my* part in this?"

Zmuda's grin faded, "It's deadly serious, I'm afraid. Chief Inspector Helga Bennet of the Free City Inquisitor's Office will call you back into service later today. A brutal crime wave has broken out in low Earth orbit and beyond that, so far, we've been able to keep secret. My source in Tunis is convinced that it ties together somehow with the North African desert quandary."

"As a cop from Free City, I can't just go parading around the Sahara for no good reason," Ryo pointed out. "I would have to be invited in by the EurAfrican authorities or the Warlord Syndicate, neither of which seems likely."

"That's OK, my friend," the spy master insisted, "we have a plan for the desert in the works right now." He pointed skyward and smiled, "The Inquisitor's Office *does* have free jurisdiction in space."

Ryo's shoulders slumped, "Please don't make me leave Dilma."

"She'll be in good hands."

8. News Item: Preliminary census data released

Dateline: 5th of August, 2446; Free City, Earth

The Free City Bureau of Statistics released a tentative tally of humankind late yesterday. The Bureau has struggled mightily for nearly ten years to fulfill the many requests for census information from both the Free City Prime Minister's Office and the Warlord Syndicate.

No accurate or concise accounting of our lowly species has been produced since the Human Census of 2140, which produced the staggering count of 15,258,195,387 just before the protracted slaughter of the Second Amero-Asian War.

The current estimate outlined in the Bureau of Statistics Daily Postings is just short of one billion at 992,231,613.

Bureau statisticians took great pains to note that the destruction last year of the crowded EurAfrican capital city of Arusha with an estimated population of 8,924,115 would have pushed the tally just over the one billion mark.

Human populations were last at this level in 1804, more than 640 years ago.

History Professor Swarna Jabuki at Free City University believes that human population numbers ebbed at a paltry 45 million several decades after the War. Jabuki suggests that the current brisk growth is mainly due to concerted efforts to produce clones mainly in EurAfrica, AmerAsia and Free City.

To the surprise of very few, our fair city is now ranked as the second most populous burg at 1,276,322. The number breaks down to 863,571 natural born, 373,545 sequential clones and 39,206 non-sequential and "other" clones. There are, of course, no serfs or slaves in Free City since the city charter deemed all such unfortunates to be free citizens in 2246.

Humankind's reigning metropolis for crowds is currently Tunis in EurAfrica at 1,513,783. The breakdown is as such: 1,098,751 serfs, 401,956 slaves, 9,036 Feudal or Slave Masters and 4,040 free "others." EurAfrica does not keep statistics that detail natural births and clonings.

9. Reluctant restraint

Chief Inspector Helga Bennet glanced up as Ryo strolled into her office.

"Mr. Trop," an uncommon smile darted across her craggy face, "apparently our mutual friend, Lieutenant Zmuda has convinced you of the atrociousness of recent developments."

"Yes," Ryo nodded glumly, "the African desert enigma is nearly unbelievable and would certainly be a tremendous step backwards for humanity, I'm afraid."

She frowned for several seconds, "Fortunately that nettlesome matter is in the hands of the CRAMP and not the Inquisitor's Office."

Helga produced three glossy color photos and spread them out amongst the clutter on her ancient desk.

Ryo winced at the bloody images.

"There has been a series of unsolved murders involving Space Debris Salvage operators." She tapped on one especially gruesome photo, "This unfortunate trio was dismembered and scattered around the midget grappler tug *Lady Luck* in orbit around the Moon."

Helga fingered a second image; "These gentlemen succumbed to blunt force trauma as the result of an ambush outside of a bar at Mariner's Station on Mars."

Ryo studied the photos, "Why haven't I heard about these misdoings in the News?"

"We've managed to keep this crime wave secret," she gathered up the pictures and slipped them back into her desk, "the Prime Minister himself clamped a gag order on the investigations at the urging of Zmuda."

"Mmm, that *is* big."

The steely old woman nodded, "There seems to be some tenuous evidence that this is somehow connected to what is transpiring in the Sahara."

Ryo sighed, "And all of this led to the Prime Minister issuing Edict 343?"

She stared unnervingly at him for several seconds, "That is correct."

His shoulders slumped under the weight of the recent revelations, "Alright; I'm back in."

"I assumed that you would be," Helga tapped out a line or two on her desktop interface. "You will meet a talented young friend and a prickly old Celtic gentleman tomorrow morning at 6 AM

58

sharp in the Law Enforcement hanger at the Ballyshannon Space Port. You will likely be away from Free City for two or three days, plan accordingly."

Ryo grimaced at the assignment.

"Edict 343 is in full effect for this investigation," she forewarned him, "you may use whatever means necessary, legal or otherwise, lethal or benign, ethical or not to clear up this unfortunate matter. I assured the Prime Minister just this morning that I would trust no one but you for this unprecedented and risky assignment."

He ruminated for a time on her dictate, "Will Dilma be in any danger?"

Helga twitched slightly at his question, "The CRAMP will apparently be looking after her."

• • •

When he heard Commander Frédéric Rameau returning from the staff meeting down the hallway the mute slave abruptly stopped mopping the floor in the little office and withdrew with his cleaning supplies.

The slave warily glanced sideways as he left the room, Commander Rameau sneered back in contempt at the minor impertinence.

Torn From On High

The tall, thin twenty-five year-old drudge lugged the mop and bucket to the janitor's closet and washed up. With the likely approval of the Building 17 Slave Master, he'd be done for the day.

Forty-five minutes later the slave trudged back into his tiny room in Domestic Servitude Housing Block 43. He busied himself for ten minutes or so tiding up his solitary quarters until he was certain that no one else was prowling about in the sparsely occupied building.

Great effort had been expended by many others to secretly place him into the position as the General Facilities slave for Rameau's office.

He pushed open the rickety wooden shutters. Just outside in the wide and dust-blown courtyard, hung on a long wire rope, were his recently hand-washed clothes.

The laundry belonging to several other slaves fluttered about on similar lines much further down the side of the wide building, but none possessed a clothesline that was quite like his.

As nearly everyone did in the dilapidated slave quarters, the man climbed through his window and stood in the courtyard to survey his desiccated garments. The baggy and ill-fitting pants and the tattered shirts were merely a disguise for the true purpose of his unusual clothesline.

Intentionally fastened upside-down at the very end where the line attached to the building at a fat ceramic insulator was a particularly ragged pair of pants. He slipped his thin fingers into the front left pocket and switched off the tiny device that had been painstakingly woven into the apparently worthless garment.

The clothesline strung across the courtyard in the Domestic Servitude Housing Block was in reality a secret and deceptively simple radio transmission antenna.

The slave reached up and unfastened the four clips that held his pants in place on the line. He stuffed the one clip that contained the thin transmission wire down into the leg of the pants before he removed the stiff, dry garb from the line. He gathered up his other items and returned to his room.

The man glanced down the hallway of the slave quarters before he sat on his cot with his "clean" clothes. He wasn't a slave and he certainly wasn't from this era, the man mused as he carefully reprogrammed the very simple transmitter in the pants pocket.

He'd been a Materials Engineering Doctoral Candidate at the University of Arizona in the fall of 2058, nearly four hundred years ago, when this strange turn of events had begun.

The "slave" methodically reset the transmitter and carefully tapped out the new twelve-character message in the long-forgotten cipher of the Southern New Mexico Regional variant of American Morse Code.

His grandmother had taught him the ancient telegraph code as a child one summer when he had complained of boredom during the long respite from school. It had been an idle curiosity then, now it might well be instrumental in the salvation of humanity.

In college an unusually insistent Genetics researcher had tracked him down and offered him a great deal of money to participate in a secret cloning experiment. He had reluctantly agreed and was sedated for the scanning process. He awoke 388 years later and 8,500 kilometers away with a new body in a clandestine lab at Free City University.

Now he was a spy.

The brownish tone of his skin and his profuse wavy black hair made him appear to be of Arabic descent when in reality he was Hispanic, a racial designation that no longer existed with the virtual extinction of humans in North America.

Lieutenant Zmuda had decided that his unusual

speech patterns from the twenty-first century American Southwest would arouse the attention of the perpetually suspicious EurAfrican Military personnel. A long-acting paralyzing drug was injected into his vocal cords to render him speechless.

He'd then been "sold" several times by cooperative and well-bribed Slavers in Mogadishu to muddle his origins. Being from the twenty-first century meant that his DNA was untraceable which further clouded his past.

The mute slave wadded up the recently dried garments and plunged them into the cloudy water of his washtub. He then climbed through the window and rehung the damp clothes on the line. Just before he finished the task, he slipped his fingers again into the tattered pants pocket and restarted the transmitter.

The twelve-character message would take hours to send using the especially narrow bandwidth allowed by the unusually low radio frequency employed by the tiny transmitter.

If someone casually dialed a receiver to the rarely used band, the message would most likely be mistaken for naturally occurring interference.

He would let the transmitter loop the message continuously for three days; its receipt was absolutely vital.

Hopefully his counterpart across the Mediterranean narrows in Sicily would pick up the transmission and promptly forward the message to Zmuda.

Tomorrow as the "mute slave" he'd again snoop through Commander Rameau's office for more information.

• • •

She had a job!

Sabra MacFarland smiled as she bumped along in the city transport as she headed back to the dingy little apartment that she shared with her sister and three others.

Sabra hadn't particularly wanted the distraction of gainful employment, but the money and the opportunity had proven to be irresistible.

Her new employer had authorized an advance of five hundred Units for what seemed like a ridiculously easy job that she probably would have done for free.

As she stared out of the transport windows at the drizzly early evening city, Sabra fidgeted with the thick stack of credentials that her boss had given to her to authorize her employment.

Suddenly she had money and some real standing!

10. News Item: Final Bicentennial parade scheduled

Dateline: 6th of August, 2446; Free City, Earth

The Free City Bicentennial Committee announced that Sunday, the 26th of August, would be the date of the final parade through our fair city. Mayor Lily Borja encouraged all citizens to participate in the event either as participants or as spectators.

As with the mammoth opening day pageant, the parade will begin at 1 PM at the City Hall Plaza and meander down several streets past the University towards Roscommon Park. The event will culminate at the War Atrocities Monument with speeches and a fireworks show at 9 PM.

Anticipating a massive turnout for the historic event, the Prime Minister has declared the 26th of August to be an official holiday for all but the most vital workers.

Both the Free City University Student Union and the Enlightenment Crusade have urged their members to wear elaborate costumes. Several downtown businesses indicated that they would award prizes to marchers for creative or thought-provoking attire.

The Bicentennial Committee is projecting that the event will be the single largest gathering in city history.

11. The death ship

Ryo stared out of the curved cockpit window of the Low Earth Orbit Class Patrol ship.

The trio had been dispatched from the Law Enforcement hanger at Free City's Ballyshannon Space Port about three hours ago and since then had been chasing down the immense salvage vessel.

But the hoped-for rendezvous with the apparently abandoned ship was considerably behind schedule.

"I don't see it yet," twenty-seven year-old Fiefdom Liaison Agent and recently certified Attack Craft Pilot Keira Norton scowled as she glanced between the wide sweep radar screen and the window.

Their timeworn passenger chortled at the young pilot's difficulties, "The *Billikin* is such a huge heap of rubbish that it will be hard to miss her, my dear.

Ryo smiled at the crusty ninety-seven year-old codger who sat behind them in the passenger's seat.

"Tell me Seamus, how many years were you the Engineer on the *Billikin*?"

"Oh, I don't know," the rickety old man stroked his white whiskers in thought, "I reckon at least a half-century beginning way back in 2370. A few years after the ship's owners made Takahashi Captain, they finally released me from my servitude. Mmm; that was in 2422, so over fifty years."

"That's quite a feat of endurance," Keira commented. "Are you proud of the time that you spent on the *Billikin*?"

"Heaven's no, child!" the old man snorted.

"That ship is an infernal piece of dog crap held together mainly by scrap wire and substandard welds. The miserly owners and the greedy captain never spent a quarter Unit more than they had to on that floating junk pile."

The straitlaced young woman blushed at the declaration by the salty spaceman.

• • •

Just as Seamus had said, Ryo wryly noted, the *Billikin* was indeed an immense floating scrap heap.

There were dozens of house-sized cast-offs from humanity's nearly five hundred year presence in Low Earth orbit fastened willy-nilly to the huge vessel. More than a few presumably dysfunctional satellites had been stuffed under a giant loose fitting net that stretched across one side of the *Billikin*. Scores of crushed and crumpled propellant tanks were lashed together with steel cables near the stern of the ship. Colossal doodads and gizmos were moored everywhere.

That amount of scrap material piled together anywhere on Earth would have been impressive; in the difficult environment of space, it was quite remarkable.

A warning buzzer interrupted Ryo's thoughts.

Keira frowned, "Well; this is a problem."

She adjusted several settings on the patrol craft's instrument panel.

"The *Billikin's* automated docking interface has apparently malfunctioned."

Ryo grinned, "After the trials and tribulations of our little expedition to the Asteroid Belt last year, manually docking with a salvage ship in Low Earth Orbit should be easy for you."

"I guess so," she replied reluctantly.

"See that?" Seamus's bony finger pointed towards the vessel, "Somebody has meddled with the docking ring hatch doors."

Torn From On High

"How are we going to get on board?"

"Not to worry, child," the old passenger answered. "I know of a rarely used auxiliary hatch that enters into the engine room."

After skirting around the ship, they came upon the small hatch. Keira eased the patrol craft into place with no small bit of advice from Seamus.

The threesome pried open the door.

Ryo stopped his cohorts just inside the silent engine room.

"We have no idea what's been lurking about on the *Billikin*; so don't take any chances."

Seamus frowned and Keira slowly nodded.

"You two check over the engine room. I'm going up to the bridge."

• • •

He certainly was dead, Ryo noted as he studied the Captain's body.

Takahashi had been beaten and staked-out like a most unfortunate specimen in a deranged bug collection.

The old Inspector called down the alleyway to

his companions.

Keira floated warily into the Captain's sleeping compartment.

"OH! That's terrible!" she cringed as she stared at the disturbing crime scene.

Ryo poked halfheartedly at the body that was splayed out like a wide 'X' against the thin sheet metal partition wall. Stout wire encircled both ankles and one wrist, which held the body in what would have been an excruciating position, had the victim been alive.

A long and very slender dagger had been driven through Takahashi's left palm and well into the thin wall behind him to complete the 'X' arrangement of the limbs.

"How did he die?" Keira whispered.

Ryo studied the corpse for several seconds. "The autopsy will tell for sure."

He tapped tentatively at the side of the dead man's neck just below his left ear. "I suspect that this has something to do with it."

A small black hole, no larger than a good-sized mole, was centered on what appeared to be an odd reddish-gray bulge that stretched from the ear lobe to the shoulder.

"This is some sort of entrance wound."

Ryo pried the rigor mortis stiffened carcass forward and peered at the back of the neck.

"DON'T LOOK," he cautioned his cohort.

"There's a gaping hole at the base of his skull."

Keira winced.

"There isn't any splatter behind him, so it didn't happen in here."

He let loose the body and it floated back against the wall.

"I suspect that he was incapacitated elsewhere and then brought in here to be put on display for some reason."

Seamus nudged his way past Keira.

"It's a sign," the old man solemnly intoned as he studied the remains.

"Of what?" Ryo asked.

"The dagger through the palm; I guess the bastard had it coming."

Keira stared at the razor-sharp blade, "What does it mean, Seamus?"

"Hoodlums and gangsters have used it for years," the old man shook his head. "It means 'stop stealing my stuff,' or some such nonsense."

"Intimidation and perhaps retribution," Ryo frowned, "but I suspect that this ghastly tableau was meant as a warning to someone else."

Keira shuddered, "He was murdered to teach others a lesson?"

"So it seems," Seamus nodded.

"Well;" Ryo sighed, "to catch the thugs who are responsible, I'm afraid that we are going to have to play along with this barbaric game until they reveal their hand."

• • •

The trio carefully searched the vessel for hours and located the many corpses of the crewmembers of the *Billikin*.

All had been gruesomely murdered but none of the nine others were displayed like the Captain.

With Seamus's help, Keira sorted through the ship's manifest and cross-referenced the names with the bodies scattered around the vessel.

"Someone is missing," she tapped at the display screen.

Ryo and Seamus studied the log.

"A Retrieval Specialist named Nathan Briggs."

"Yeah; I remember Nate," Seamus nodded. "He was a Serf from EurAfrica just like me. The poor dog was stuck taking a beat up old runabout out to wrangle promising debris. It's the toughest job on the *Billikin*. Maybe he just snapped and went on a killing spree."

"I wonder," Ryo frowned, "where is Mr. Briggs now?"

Seamus turned to the Inspector, "I did notice that the retrieval runabout is missing."

After nearly a minute of careful thought, Ryo finally spoke, "I think for now we have to assume that Nate Briggs is a prime suspect in these murders."

• • •

An hour later at Ryo's request, Keira sent out an All-Points Bulletin that requested any available information about Nate Briggs while the men busied themselves elsewhere.

When her task was completed, she took one long last look at the Captain's body before she sought out her cohorts.

74

Keira shivered as she floated down the eerie passageway of the derelict vessel.

The young woman was certain that she would always remember the *Billikin* as the 'death ship.'

• • •

During the prolonged interval as they waited for the Free City Coroner to arrive at the *Billikin* and take over the crime scene, Ryo held a hushed conversation with Seamus amongst the clutter of the aft cargo bay.

When Keira had come upon the two men, the old Inspector had tersely and uncharacteristically warned her off. It would be best for everyone if she knew nothing of the impending trickery.

After she had reluctantly left them, Ryo continued.

He pointed at the text on the screen of his communication device, "You're OK with this?"

Seamus nodded, "I'm a worn-out old man; I don't really have anything to lose."

"Alright then, let the deception begin." Ryo pressed the 'send' button and the deed was done.

The two men brooded in silence for several seconds.

Torn From On High

The pleasant chirp of Ryo's communication device broke the unwelcome reflection on the day's horrifying events.

It was Chief Inspector Helga Bennet.

She began without formalities, "We received word about ten minutes ago that Nate Briggs, or at least what's left of him, has been located. I'm sending you the location information. Tend to this right away."

The screen changed to flashing red text.

Ryo frowned at the coordinates, "This is an odd place for a Space Debris Retrieval Specialist."

12. News Item: Slaughter in orbit!

Dateline: 7th of August, 2446; Aboard the salvage ship Billikin in Low Earth Orbit.

Adrift high above the heads of the lowly humans on Earth is a most disturbing crime scene.

Free City Investigators were called in to sift through the bloody mess onboard the salvage ship *Billikin* in Low Earth Orbit late yesterday. The immense floating boneyard of space debris has the grisly distinction of being the site of the largest mass murder onboard a near-Earth vessel in over eighty years.

Rumors have spread in the past few days that some sort of terrible fate had befallen the good ship and crew but none had predicted the gruesomeness of the deed.

While investigators at the Free City Inquisitor's Office remain maddeningly mute about the slaughter, an eyewitness account has surfaced from another source.

"The butchery was quite disturbing," reported ninety-seven year-old Free City resident Seamus Nelson who was a former crewman onboard the *Billikin*. The retired Ship's Engineer accompanied investigators when they first discovered the massacre on the marooned vessel.

"There were dreadful signs of torture and one body was ritualistically displayed," confided Mr. Nelson about the horrific massacre. He indicated that the investigators had rapidly pieced together many details at the crime scene and that arrests were likely soon.

This morning the Space Salvage Cartel, which has been supplied with significant quantities of scrap materials in the past from the *Billikin*, offered a hefty reward of fifty thousand Standard Units to anyone who aids in the capture of the mass murderers.

Those with any information about the atrocities onboard the *Billikin* are urged to contact the Free City Inquisitor's Office at once.

13. The hired companion

Sabra sat stiffly on the hard wooden bench in the hushed and nearly empty hallway just outside of the office. Many of the trinkets and baubles crowded around her low-cut attire jangled softly as she moved.

She certainly was quite a spectacle at the subdued and straitlaced institution.

The receptionist at the Connaught School for Disadvantaged Girls had made no effort to hide her distaste for Sabra when she had arrived nearly an hour earlier. Now she waited to be called into the office of the Head of the School.

Sabra thought it was amusing early on; sitting nervously, as she had occasionally done during her own childhood, to be scolded for some minor transgression by the principal or head teacher, but this was different: she was an adult now and was being generously compensated to tend to this particular matter.

Sabra silently considered whether it would be appropriate to mention the stuffy and inhospitable treatment that she'd received to her esteemed employer.

He would likely be displeased, but with whom? Sabra or the staff of the Connaught School?

Torn From On High

Two days earlier, the mysterious redheaded woman had reappeared at the *Investigations Into Alternative Lifestyles 501* classroom at the University. She had pulled Sabra aside before the instruction had begun and told her of a rare opportunity for a well-paid job.

When Sabra had dithered and expressed a reluctance to take on the responsibility, the fiery redhead just snickered, "The hundred Units that you owe me says you'll accept the job, sweetie."

Thwarted by her lack of funds, Sabra followed the woman out of the classroom and down to the Student Union.

They nudged their way through the crowd at the sprawling food court and slipped into a small cafe. There in the back, seated alone as he thumbed through a thick stack of documents was a graying older man. He could have been a professor or senior researcher at the University, Sabra judged by his appearance and detached manner.

The redhead stood politely at the table awaiting the old man's attention with her hand clasped firmly around Sabra's wrist.

After several seconds, he looked up from the document that he'd been studying, "Yes?"

"Inspector Trop of the Inquisitor's Office?" the woman inquired.

Sabra had winced at the question; was she about to start working for a cop?

"Please;" the man smiled warmly, "call me Ryo."

The woman bowed a bit, "Fair enough."

She tugged Sabra to the forefront, "Ryo, this is Miss Sabra MacFarland and she is most enthusiastically seeking the hired companion position for your twelve-year-old child."

The man grinned wryly at the introduction and beckoned Sabra to sit.

The mysterious woman hovered nearby for a minute or so before dashing off.

In an endearing and slightly befuddled way, Ryo explained to Sabra about his faltering efforts as the guardian of the young girl. The Connaught School was tending to her education and he was nurturing her as best he could in a fatherly way, but what she really needed now was a world-wise young woman as a sort of surrogate older sister.

Ryo had stared pleadingly into her eyes at one point, "Dilma could really use the help."

And so, with only a bit more prompting, she had taken the job without even meeting the child.

The 'work' sounded absurdly easy for the amount of pay that he had offered. Sabra would fetch Dilma each day at school and then tend to her from 3 in the afternoon until 7 in the evening, entertaining her in any way that she saw fit. Occasionally she would look after Dilma for several days if an investigation took Ryo away from the city.

They were to avoid trouble "if possible," Ryo had winked. However he would not be upset, he assured her, if they engaged in minor mischief.

Ryo tapped out an advance payment of five hundred Units for the first week's wages on a payment interface and handed her a thick stack of documents with the particulars and permissions to pick up Dilma at the Connaught School in two day's time.

"Be aware," Ryo cautioned, "that Dilma is quite clever but *terribly* naive."

• • •

Sabra stared with icy annoyance at the prim old biddy as she meticulously examined the credentials.

The Head of the Connaught School had kept her waiting for over two hours and now seemed intent on finding some technicality to thwart Sabra in her effort to take charge of Dilma.

The stern gray woman sighed and handed the documents back to Sabra, "I don't like you."

Sabra's eyes narrowed at the comment.

Perhaps, she guessed, this was some sort of rather cruel test by the hardhearted Head of the School to discover whether she possessed the inner toughness to deal with the emotional ups and downs that twelve-year-old Dilma might present.

The old woman coldly appraised her for several seconds, "I don't like your unconventional lifestyle or appearance. I don't care for your choice in higher education. I *certainly* do not fancy your conspicuous body odor and your apparent lack of bathing."

Sabra scowled at the scolding.

"I'm afraid that your paperwork is flawlessly in order and the properly notarized instructions from Inspector Trop are quite clear," the crone huffed with annoyance, "I must turn Dilma over to a wretch that I would not trust to walk my dog."

Sabra felt a delightful surge of adrenaline; she had quietly achieved a surprising victory over the moldering and rigid woman who typified the fading old guards of single-minded morality. Sabra had, as an unashamed member of the forward thinking Enlightenment Crusade, at least temporarily, vanquished a representative of the inflexible class system of the past.

Perhaps, as she now postulated Ryo had surmised two days earlier, she would indeed make an excellent mentor for Dilma.

• • •

A rather timid looking dark-haired girl was waiting with her school supplies at the reception desk when Sabra finally left the oppressive office of the Head of the Connaught School at 4 PM.

With an uncommon air of recently hard-won self-confidence, Sabra appraised her shy young protégé.

Dilma was much smaller and thinner than Sabra had imagined; with huge sad brown eyes, a drawn angular face dappled with hundreds of faint freckles and a brushed-back mane of long, slightly rippled coffee-colored hair to frame it all.

The girl drooped dolefully down at the approach of her new nanny.

"Hi;" Sabra summoned a broad smile, "are you Dilma?"

The youngster nodded warily.

"I am Sabra. It is nice to finally meet you."

The woman held out her hand in greeting.

Dilma studied the open palm for several seconds before delicately tracing the lines and furrows of Sabra's skin with her tiny fingertips.

The girl stared up at the woman in awe.

"You're very pretty," she whispered.

"As are you."

Dilma blushed.

Sabra hoisted the youngster's school bag, "Shall we lope about the city for a few hours?"

The girl gently fingered the dozens of tiny metal medallions and beads that jingled invitingly from Sabra's colorful corset top.

The woman marveled at the child's unrestrained curiosity, "Perhaps, if Inspector Trop sees fit, we will find you some clothes like these in a few weeks."

Dilma eagerly nodded at the suggestion.

"But there's just one thing, Sabra."

"What is it, sweetie?"

The girl produced a radiant smile for the first time, "*Everyone* calls him Ryo."

Sabra smiled as they headed out into the cold breeze of the city, "So I've heard."

14. News Item: Kufuzu alive?

Dateline: 8th of August, 2446; Nairobi, EurAfrica, Earth

Tantalizing rumors have surfaced in the back alleys and drinking establishments of Nairobi that Daniel Kufuzu, the Benevolent and Exalted Fourth Warlord of EurAfrica *may* have, by some unexplained miracle, survived last year's destruction of Arusha.

Although the EurAfrican authorities in our de facto capital of New Rome steadfastly maintain that Kufuzu was vaporized along with nine million others by the antimatter bomb that destroyed the former capital on the Maasai Steppes, the pervasiveness and fervor of this street-buzz begs for further investigation.

Speculation ranges from the reasonable suggestions that our beloved leader was, in fact, recuperating from a minor malady at the seaside palace in Morocco during the blast to the ludicrous jabber that the Exalted One has somehow been recloned as a fully cognitive adult in a secret desert laboratory.

All rumors suggest that Daniel Kufuzu will soon return to his rightful status as Warlord of

EurAfrica and sweep aside the bleating
bureaucrats in New Rome that have allowed the
lowly serfs and slaves in our doleful Fiefdom to
grumble aloud about their situation.

With the current untenable turmoil in the streets
and workhouses of Nairobi, that bold action
cannot come soon enough.

15. New Grytviken

With the re-entry thrusters no longer needed,
Keira engaged the dive brakes and the thin,
turbulent air of the upper Mesosphere began to
buffet the compact patrol craft.

The drag caused by the relentless collision
between the ethereal air molecules and the wide,
flat projections would greatly slow the ship in
the coming minutes causing it to fall out of orbit
and dissipate over thirty million watt-hours of
kinetic energy along the way.

Ryo cringed from the steadily increasing
battering inflicted upon him by the shuddering
craft. The rough treatment of re-entry was an
unwelcome requirement for the return to Earth;
thankfully not one that he'd often had to endure.

Seamus groaned at the steadily increasing
punishment and muttered a Gaelic prayer for
salvation.

Between slight adjustments to the controls, Keira
chuckled at the angst of her elderly companions.
"What is it with old gents and re-entry?"

The rapidly increasing g-forces that pressed
down on the men prevented either of them from
answering.

Torn From On High

After many minutes, the automatic descent program slowly retracted the dive brakes and engaged the aerodynamic control surfaces.

"Alright," Keira finally told the men, "we're at about a thirty thousand meters above the Pacific just north of the equator."

She tapped at the controls for several seconds. "Hang on; we're about to veer southeast for a three hour trip to our objective."

The young pilot studied the particulars about their destination.

"Hopefully we have three survival suits onboard. It's going to be dark, windy and very cold when we get there."

• • •

"I don't see any place to land," Ryo scowled as he stared out at the night-shrouded estuary.

Keira looped around Cumberland East Bay for a second look, "I have the coordinates and there should be some sort of landing lights."

She frowned at the difficulties.

"There it is!" Seamus pointed to the left.

A single dim spotlight seemed to be tracking

them from the ground, wavering between faint and nearly invisible, the beam appeared to be directed at them from a handheld lamp.

Keira followed the beckoning light.

They hovered a few hundred meters over the thin shaft of light.

A shadowy figure tilted the spotlight towards the ground and illuminated a miniscule flat gray patch of gravel.

"Apparently that's the landing pad," Ryo shrugged.

"We *did not* practice this sort of thing in flight school," Keira grumbled.

The patrol craft groaned and wobbled as it settled slightly askew on the small, rough rectangle.

Seamus passed two bright orange survival suits to his companions.

The threesome shimmied into the tight-fitting garments in the cramped cabin. Both Ryo and Keira spent several minutes pulling the snug hood over Seamus's head.

The three stiff and orange-clad visitors stood uncomfortably at the hatch as Ryo tapped at the locking mechanism.

Torn From On High

The door opened to an icy gust of wind.

"GOOD MORNING!" a deep and gregarious voice boomed through the darkness. "Welcome to South Georgia Island!"

• • •

Nearly twelve thousand kilometers north-northeast of the dark and windswept landing site on South Georgia Island, in a warm and secret little office at Free City University; Lieutenant Zmuda and his two cohorts considered the many implications of the morning News Item about the massacre on the *Billikin*.

"Is this a *real* story or did someone plant it in the media?" Mixion wondered.

Zmuda frowned, "Nobody should know about this yet; the Inquisitor's Office is most likely still going over the crime scene."

Jasper sighed as he read the dispatch over the Lieutenant's shoulder; "It sure seems to put this Seamus Nelson fellow in peril."

"Ah;" Zmuda finally tapped in victory at the News Item, "this is Ryo Trop's work."

He turned to the two other CRAMP agents, "Find out everything that you can about a ninety-seven year-old former Engineer named Mr.

Seamus Nelson who currently resides in Free City."

Mixion and Jasper nodded in unison.

"I suspect," Zmuda grimaced, "that others are doing the same thing right now."

• • •

The big man gleefully dished another steaming pancake onto Ryo's plate.

"Thank you Luis, I think that will about do it for me," the Investigator groaned as he contemplated eating what would be his fifth serving.

Both Keira and Seamus had a similarly bloated look as the groggy threesome sat around the breakfast table in the cluttered white cottage on the wind-blown bluff.

Their host gazed attentively at his guests.

"It's just that I haven't seen anyone for over five months," Luis added gloomily, "at least no one alive."

Keira frowned, "You're all alone on South Georgia Island?"

Luis nodded, "Yes. It's just me and Moresby who

tend to matters during the off season at New Grytviken."

"Moresby?" Seamus asked.

"He's the ancient gray tabby cat that the previous Harbor Master left behind when I took up the job twelve years ago."

Ryo nodded between bites, "What exactly do you do in this lovely but thoroughly frozen South Atlantic outpost?"

"South Georgia Island is technically part of the Grand Eternal Fiefdom of AmerAsia, I don't think that anyone else would want it, but it's the AmerAsian Interior Ministry in Buenos Aires that pays the bills to keep the harbor open."

"Open for what?" Seamus scoffed.

Luis beamed at the curmudgeonly old man, "I've often wondered that myself. The original village of Grytviken was a British and Norwegian whaling port. When that died out, it was a sparsely used way station for cruise ships destined for the Antarctic. Now the Interior Ministry has some hopes that Cumberland Bay could eventually be a supply port for Antarctic mineral extraction."

"New Grytviken?" Keira glanced around the room, "These quaint old relics aren't from the original village?"

"Well:" Luis hedged, "more or less. The settlement was flooded when the sea level rose a few hundred years ago. They moved nearly everything up on the bluff and renamed it New Grytviken."

"Everything?" Ryo smiled.

"Yeah; even the old cemetery with Sir Ernest Shackleton's grave, it's still the only real claim to fame here."

"Speaking of bodies," Ryo stared up at their host, "I understand that you discovered one a few days ago."

Luis's expression darkened, "Yes; the poor fellow is down in one of the boathouses."

• • •

A frigid squall raked merciless across the foursome.

"So!" Ryo shouted above the roar of the wind, "how did you come upon Mr. Briggs' body?"

Once again in their orange survival suits, the three visitors trudged long with Luis as they labored towards the harbor.

"One of my duties at New Grytviken is that of the Harbor Master of Cumberland East Bay."

95

Torn From On High

A sudden gust of icy wind caused Seamus to wobble precariously until Luis and Keira steadied the old man.

"Twice a week on Tuesdays and Fridays I take a small grappler tug around the perimeter of the bay and then through the length of the two shipping lanes." He pressed forward against the wind, "If I find anything floating around that could be a hazard to navigation, I tow it to the harbor and secure it."

"Do you find much stuff?" Keira yelled.

He nodded, "I found a basketball from a girl's school in Manila a few years ago, it's up in the cottage somewhere."

Luis led them down a long creaky dock, "Mostly its just driftwood logs and stray fishing nets, a few years ago I spent days tending to a capsized speed boat that had strayed away from the marina at Governor's Bay in New Zealand which is over fifteen thousand kilometers away!"

"Mildly valuable cast-offs," Seamus smiled, "that sounds to me like space debris salvage."

They stopped at the tall, waterside edge of the dock and stared at the huge mangled silver and black cylindrical object that bobbed in the choppy water as it pulled impatiently against the stout cables that moored it.

Their host pointed to the battered and burned object that was at least twice the size of his cottage, "This monstrosity was floating just outside of the bay about a week ago."

Seamus studied the dented and scorched artifact, "It's the upper stage of an old Y69 rocket booster, I've seen a dozen or so, although they're usually in much better shape in Low Earth Orbit."

Ryo tilted his head in confusion, "I thought that nothing could survive the inferno of an uncontrolled plunge to Earth."

"It depends on a lot of factors such as the angle of re-entry and the composition of the object," Seamus pointed to booster, "but the most important thing is size."

Luis nodded, "There's a good thirty tons of titanium, aluminum and PlastiStruct in that thing."

"As interesting as this relic is," Ryo shivered, "what does it have to do with Mr. Nathan Briggs?"

Luis frowned, "Tangled up in the stainless steel plumbing for the rocket engines, fairly well protected from the heat of re-entry, I found what I thought was a helmet and the upper half of a space suit."

The visitors followed him into a tidy old boathouse.

Finally out of the frigid wind, Luis continued, "Something like that would be a great novelty to show off to tourists: the space suit that found its way from orbit to New Grytviken."

They stood shivering together around a shipping crate that was the size of a large trunk.

Luis lifted off the cover and Keira flinched in horror.

The remnants of the space suit contained the charred and mutilated remains of a man.

Seamus whispered a Gaelic prayer, Ryo stared ashen-faced at the body and Keira spun around and vomited.

"Gruesome; I know," Luis solemnly noted, "but at least the cold keeps the smell down."

After several minutes of reflection over the corpse, Ryo asked the obvious question, "How did you discover that this was Nate Briggs?"

"I planned to give the poor bloke a proper burial in the cemetery during the summer when the ground finally thaws out. I felt that it was only right to put his given name on the grave marker," Luis gently pulled the glove away from the
98

body's hand, "so I slid his fingertip over a payment interface for a good half an hour until it finally produced his name."

Keira dry heaved and covered her eyes at the sight of the distorted and blackened hand.

"When I contacted the Free City Bureau of Records to register the death, they told me that an Investigator from the Inquisitor's Office was on the way."

"Thank you for that, Luis." Ryo glanced up at Keira and pointed to the door. "You may want to wait outside, sweetheart."

She nodded in relief and hurried away.

"In a few minutes I'd like for you to pack Mr. Briggs for transport and we will take his remains back to the Coroner's Office in Free City."

Ryo gingerly unfastened the helmet and, with the skills of an Investigator who had seen hundreds of bodies, he carefully studied the back of Nate Briggs' neck.

Ryo turned to Seamus, "Would you say that we saw this type of wound on Captain Takahashi?"

The old man winced, "Yes."

The Investigator lingered over the corpse for a

time before finally returning the cover to the shipping crate.

He stared at Seamus with a look of consternation; "Let's just hope that I don't find the same sort of trauma on your corpse in the next few days."

16. The turbulence just below the placid surface

Luis stood alone in the gloom as the icy wind howled across the landing area in New Grytviken. Fifty meters away the sleek patrol craft shuddered as the launch thrusters came to life.

He waved one last time to Keira and Ryo through the wide, curved cockpit window as they busied themselves preparing the ship for departure. Luis caught glimpses of Seamus behind the two pilots.

The old man returned his wave.

The thrusters roared mightily and the patrol craft lifted skyward. At about three hundred meters, the ship rotated slowly to the north. The aerodynamic control surfaces reconfigured for high-speed flight and the big main engine throttled up.

The ship dashed away with a rumbling sonic boom that echoed between the cliffs that surrounded New Grytviken.

Luis stood for many minutes in the gusty twilight of South Georgia Island. For a time he watched

the rapidly receding red and blue marker lights
of the patrol craft as the ship raced toward the
northern horizon and then he just stared wistfully
into the distance at the scowling gray storm
clouds.

He was alone again.

Luis was shaken from his doleful introspection
by an especially surly blast of freezing wind.

The man gathered his thoughts and trudged back
towards his little white cottage on the bluff
above the harbor. He wasn't likely to see another
soul until the supply ship sailed into Cumberland
East Bay sometime in mid-March.

A light smattering of snow swirled around as he
made his way up the path.

The warm lights of his tiny home shone through
the windows.

Luis smiled a bit as he ascended the five frost-
covered steps to the front door.

There sitting patiently in the front window
awaiting his return was Moresby, his steadfast
gray tabby cat.

• • •

S F Chapman

"This afternoon," Sabra grinned impishly as she met Dilma at the reception desk at the Connaught School, "I'd like to take you over to Roscommon Park."

The skittery little girl's eyes grew huge at the prospect of a grand adventure with her new nanny.

"The park?"

"Yeah, it'll be great fun." Sabra shouldered the girl's school bag; "The Bicentennial Exposition will only be open for a few more weeks, so if you don't see it now, you probably never will."

Dilma raced ahead through the lobby and pulled open the heavy front doors. The two glided together down the wide stone staircase to the busy street.

They strolled hand in hand on the crowded sidewalk.

"How was your school day, kitten?" the woman asked.

Dilma skipped several steps before answering; "We studied about the Greeks in the morning, played four-square at lunch break and worked on some couplet poetry in the afternoon."

She stopped and cocked her head, "What about

you, Sabra?"

The woman smiled at the earnest question,
"Well; after I dropped you off at school, I
trudged on over to the University and sat through
my *Historical Rebellions* lecture, which was
deadly dull. Then I went back to your apartment
and tidied up a bit. I had a snack and took a bath.
After that I called Ryo's office to see if they had
any idea as to when he'd be back in Free City.
They didn't, so it looks like I'll sleep at your
apartment again tonight and get you off to school
in the morning."

Dilma nodded with glee at the happy prospect.

"Oh, I almost forgot," Sabra mentioned when
they stopped at the corner to wait for a
westbound transport. The woman retrieved the
wide bejeweled headband decorated with a
bright silvery concha of an eagle from her head,
"this is for you."

Dilma stared in amazement at the offering. Her
fingers slid appraisingly over the bone and brass
beadwork for several seconds.

Sabra grinned at her awestruck charge, "Let's put
it on you, sweetie."

She adjusted the clasp and slipped it onto the
youngster's head.

Dilma's face glowed with the attention of the idolized woman and the joy of receiving the newfound treasure.

"There;" Sabra stepped back and admired her gangly young companion, "you look splendid. You'd fit right in with the Enlightenment Crusaders."

The girl blushed at the praise, "Thank you, Sabra."

• • •

Tariq trotted into the coolness of the desert cave and bowed in deference to the Warlord.

As was his habit, the recently recloned raven-skinned leader leisurely finished up the final few morsels of his lunch before he acknowledged Tariq's arrival.

The ruler finally dabbed his lips with the sleeve of his sweat-stained cotton shirt, "What is it, my servant?"

"Oh Exalted One;" Tariq intoned, "a courier from Tunis delivered a message from My Master, Commander Frédéric Rameau at the Military Base."

The Warlord scowled a bit, "Did you murder the courier after he gave you the message?"

"Yes;" Tariq nodded, "as per your command, my leader. The message-bearer is dead and will be unable to reveal our location to your adversaries."

"Excellent," the Warlord smiled. "What is the information that Commander Rameau wished for me to know?"

Tariq stared into the forbidding eyes of the man for several seconds before he answered. The act was impertinent and might well result in his own swift demise, but Tariq felt that he *had* to see the man's first reaction to the startling news.

"My Master..," Tariq stammered, "...has deduced who is responsible...for the murder of your most beloved third wife, Sophia."

The Warlord's face darkened into a hateful mask of vengeance.

"How is Rameau using this information?" the man finally growled.

Tariq quivered as he contemplated the smoldering ruler, "My Master has set in place an effort to kill the rogue."

• • •

Dilma dipped her thin fingers into the trickling water of the Commemoration Day fountain in the park.

It had been a marvelous adventure for her young charge, Sabra noted as she watched the girl.

Dilma had eagerly tried every strange variation of food that they had come upon at the Free City Bicentennial Exposition. She especially liked the spicy Thai/Martian fusion fare that was available at a brightly lit booth near the Warlord Syndicate Pavilion.

Sabra stopped to wait while the girl picked a few stray leaves from the pool of water at the base of the fountain.

She was quite a sight, the woman grinned. When they had first arrived at the Exposition nearly four hours ago, Dilma pointed in great glee at several other youngsters sporting colorful face paintings. Sabra located a booth that applied the makeup and Dilma sat nearly motionless for ten minutes while the artist transformed her thin freckly face into a fair facsimile of a stylized blue butterfly.

Sabra had added to the merry illusion by buying a matching blue-feathered boa for the girl.

Dilma finished up at the fountain and skipped to Sabra's side.

They stopped a few minutes later in the rose garden. The girl was fascinated by the profusion of soft petals that adorned the thorny old bushes.

Torn From On High

Sabra smiled when the child carefully plucked samples from several different blooms and let them flutter to the ground like a flock of tiny birds.

The two continued their stroll together through the park.

Dilma pointed to a crowd of a dozen or so people up ahead, "What are they doing over there?"

Sabra knew the somber location well but apparently her young companion did not, "Let's go see, sweetie."

They joined the solemn group at the base of War Atrocities Monument.

Nearly everyone in Free City stopped for several minutes of quiet reflection at the memorial when visiting the park. Every year on Commemoration Day people would slowly file by to lay symbolic notes to the dead at the monument.

"It seems so sad here," Dilma stared up at the woman.

"It's a way of remembering everyone who died during the Second Amero-Asian War," Sabra whispered.

Dilma tentatively touched the cold gray stone surface of the base.

"Did a lot of people die?"

"Nearly everyone, I'm afraid."

The girl grimly contemplated the symbol meant to mourn the victims of humanity's greatest folly.

"Why did it happen?" Dilma asked.

"Stupidity. Nations argued and fought; eventually almost everyone was murdered."

The girl slowly nodded with an unwelcome new understanding of the treacherous nature of humanity. Lingering just below the surface of fun and frivolity was a sinister undertow of self-destruction.

17. Revelations

Keira set the patrol craft down in a near perfect landing next to the Law Enforcement hanger at the Ballyshannon Space Port.

Ryo stared out into the darkness at the deserted facility, "Where is everyone?"

Keira glanced at the ship's clock as she toggled several switches to shut down the craft, "It's 2:13 AM, the hanger is only staffed until midnight."

"I'd like to get Nate Briggs' corpse over to the coroner's office as soon as possible," he grumbled.

Keira smiled weakly at the old Investigator, "I'll send a urgent request over to their office. They do pick ups around the clock."

The exhausted cop nodded, "Thanks; the sooner the body is hauled away to the morgue, the sooner I'll be back to my warm bed in Free City."

She twisted around in the pilot's seat and woke Seamus, "Come on old man, we need to catch the 2:30 transport back to town or we'll have to wait a couple of hours for the next one."

Seamus squinted in incomprehension at the

woman for several seconds before struggling out of his seat.

Ryo caught Keira's wrist as she stood, "Before you go, I have two requests."

She studied him with concern.

"If you'd open the cargo hatch and lower the crate with Mr. Briggs' remains to the tarmac, the coroner's men and I won't have to fumble about with that task."

"Certainly." The woman flipped a switch on the console and the low rumble of the opening cargo bay doors pervaded the ship. When the 'Hatch Open' light flashed green, she activated the cargo lift.

Keira bit her lip and turned to Ryo, "What was the second thing?"

The bone-weary Investigator glanced back at Seamus, "Walk him to his apartment and do a thorough but discreet search of the place before you leave him."

She frowned and was about to ask why.

Ryo held up his hand and stopped her, "*Don't ask, just do it.*"

"OK;" the woman frowned, "since Lev's out of

town, I'm not in any hurry to get back to my cold and lonely apartment anyway."

The exhausted threesome straggled off of the patrol craft.

Ten minutes later, Ryo watched enviously as Keira and Seamus boarded the nearly empty transport back to Free City.

At 4:03 the boxy black Free City Coroner's vehicle screeched to a stop next to the patrol craft.

The pimply-faced driver loped out and approached Ryo, "Good morning, I'm here for a pick up. Are you Inspector Trop?"

Ryo nodded in dismay, "Yeah, but the two of us won't be able to get this crate into your rig."

"It's not a problem for a change," the young man waved to the vehicle, "my boss sent me out with another guy for some reason. I would have been here sooner but I had to stop by the University to pick him up."

The side door of the transport slid open to reveal a uniformed middle-aged man who sported a wide grin.

Ryo smiled in surprise, it was Lieutenant Zmuda dressed as a Coroner's Assistant.

112

Zmuda joined the men at the crate.

"Inspector;" the Lieutenant adeptly played his part, "I'm Uloff Lebrinski, Suspicious Deaths Auxiliary Pathology Technician."

Ryo winked at his old friend; now it was his turn to fabricate a story. "We came upon this poor chap floating around off the coast and some gents in a passing fishing trawler crated him up for us."

Zmuda stroked his chin in mock dismay, "Alright, we will see what we can find out about him."

The three men lugged the heavy packing crate into the Coroner's transport.

When the box was lashed in place, Zmuda turned to the driver, "Wait here with the body, I need to get some details from Inspector Trop for the Preliminary Report."

The two older men returned to the patrol craft.

When they were finally inside the spacecraft, Ryo chortled at Zmuda, "*Uloff Lebrinski?* Where do you get these names?"

The Lieutenant grinned in reply, "We did a study at the University a few years back that proved that people will often only remember that a name is unusual but invariably couldn't actually recall what the name was."

Ryo rolled his eyes.

Zmuda's smile faded, "What's your best guess as to how Nate Briggs and the others on the *Billikin* died?"

"Murdered, or at least disabled, using some sort of new narrow-beam energy weapon. It was all quite gruesome."

The Lieutenant drummed his fingertips on the side of a bulkhead, "Well; that part seems to be falling into place, I'm afraid. The EurAfrican Commander of Covert Operations in Tunis had three handheld particle beam weapons specially produced that could really cause problems. They appear to be remarkably effective as an assassin's side arm."

"So someone has gotten a hold of one and is blasting junkmen in Low Earth Orbit?"

Zmuda winced, "So it seems."

Ryo frowned, "Bigger and better guns, that's all we need in the hands of lunatics. I'll poke around in the office in the next few days and let you know what I find out."

"Thanks." Zmuda glanced out of the cockpit window, "Do you know a Liaison Agent named

114

Hugo Mackillroy?"

"Mac?" Ryo nodded with a yawn, "Yeah; he and I have worked together off and on for years. Why did you ask?"

"He sent a message to your boss indicating that he had some vital information for me."

Ryo smiled a bit, "Mac's always turning up good leads."

"I was afraid of that."

Ryo could tell that something was amiss, "What's the problem?"

Zmuda's eyebrows arched up, "Agent Mackillroy insisted that he would *only* reveal what he knows to a top official of the CRAMP in person. Helga says that he was adamant about meeting with me in New Rome."

"Well;" Ryo nodded, "that *is* unusual but not unheard of with Mac."

The spy was visibly relieved.

"The meeting is in two days and Helga wants you to accompany me."

"Of course she does," Ryo shook his head in dismay. "I just want to relax at home and spend some time with my kid."

"After a short trip to New Rome, I promise that I will leave you alone for awhile."

• • •

The urgent "message" slowly blinked in a long string of red dots and dashes on the desktop interface screen.

Mixion stared sleepily at the characters in the warm, quiet workroom. It was 5:47 AM and she was unlucky enough to be on duty in the CRAMP office.

Lieutenant Zmuda had been anxiously awaiting dispatches from the spy at the EurAfrican Imperial Military Base in Tunis. He'd deemed the messages so vital that the communication link to the contact in Sicily had been continuously monitored for the last several weeks.

The previous three reports had been mundane: the first merely acknowledged that the tall "mute" had activated the tiny transmitter, the second confirmed that he had been working in Commander Rameau's office and the third indicated that he was able to search through documents on the Commander's desk.

Mixion refocused her flagging attention back to

116

the screen. In her current thick and heavy-eyed state she'd never be able to unravel the mishmash of flashing dots and dashes.

She sighed and withdrew several sheets of white paper and three pencils from the desk drawer. With mind-numbing concentration so as not make an error, she copied the Morse Code onto the paper.

Mixion was well-aware of the limitations of the tiny transmitter, the far less than optimal antenna and the especially narrow bandwidth, all of which meant that the message had to be absurdly short and repeated many times to increase the chances of successful communication. Errors were to be expected in the messages.

The woman retrieved the *Southern New Mexico Regional Variant of American Morse Code* reference that the spy had produced before Zmuda had sent him off to Africa. She set to work transcribing the dispatch.

A half an hour later she had finished and began studying the long string of letters and numbers earnest.

922E17221M98012E1?22?N080??E17221N08

She'd placed question marks where the symbols had been too garbled to assign a character with any certainty.

"E1" popped out right away, the letter and number combination repeated three times in the 36-character segment.

She cautiously wrote out "E17221" because the five symbols appeared together in two out of the three occurrences that started with "E1."

It was just past eight o'clock.

Mixion carefully reread the two-page appendix at the end of the Morse Code reference. 'The number one can often be misinterpreted as two,' she grinned with newfound comprehension. 'Nine and zero were often mistaken for each other. M and N have a similar problem.'

She scratched away at the message for many minutes. Mixion patiently substituted letters and numbers that were commonly misinterpreted or transposed as she rewrote the message seven different ways.

The woman finally underlined her interpretation: Probably E17221N0801?

Mixion took a deep breath and changed the question mark to the number two, producing E17221N08012.

That was it, she smiled weakly, the twelve-character combination had repeated itself at least twice in the middle of the string and in consecutive fragments at either end.

But what did it mean?

After several minutes of consternation, she tapped on the communications device and summoned Jasper from the Situation Room.

When the big man arrived, Mixion showed him the short message.

"What can you make of this, Jasper?"

Mmm; I don't know, sweetheart." He tipped his head, "The 'N' and the 'E' remind me of compass settings, but the order is wrong and I have no idea how the numbers fit in."

Mixion stared up at the big man, "There's an *order* to compass settings?"

"Yeah; I learned about it in the Boy Scouts as a kid, you start with North and move clockwise around the compass face. So North, East, South, West."

"Mmm;" Mixion glanced at the sheet, "well that helps."

She methodically recopied the message in reverse yielding 21080N12271E. "Apparently our spy was taking no chances and has decided to disguise the information further by sending it backwards."

Jasper nodded, "Add a space between the N and the 1."

Mixion complied. "Are these map coordinates?"

"I think so, but there should be decimal points in there somewhere."

"OK; I have a hunch that I want to play out." She tapped at the desktop interface screen and called up a World map. "Our spy is in Tunis, so let's start with Africa." She highlighted the section of the continent North of the equator and entered the string of numbers and letters.

Four possible locations appeared on the screen. One was in deep water off the coast, one was in dense jungle and two were in the immense Saharan Desert.

Jasper chuckled, "I think we can rule out the Atlantic and the rainforest for now."

She pointed at the screen, "Alright; we'll start with these two spots in the desert."

"One is on the border between Algeria and Mali and the other is a high desert plateau in Niger," he summarized. "Let's look at the satellite images for these sites."

120

Mixion tapped at the Algerian border coordinates and toggled the resolution to five square centimeters. "Mmm; I don't see much of anything but empty desert for twenty or thirty kilometers in any direction."

"Try the other one," Jasper suggested.

She switched to the second location and smiled, "Bingo!"

"Ruins of some sort." He squinted at the screen, "Are those people?"

Mixion zoomed in on two conspicuous orange and green striped dots. "It looks like a couple of gun-toting Desert Serfs."

He kissed the top of her head as she stared at the screen, "I'll tell the boss that we've found something interesting."

Jasper trotted off in search of the Lieutenant with a hastily made copy of the map coordinates.

Mixion slowly scanned the area that surrounded the Desert Serfs.

"I wonder what these two are doing out in the middle of nowhere?"

18. News Item:
Space salvage deaths soar

Dateline: 22nd of August, 2446; New Rome, EurAfrica, Earth

This morning the Warlord Syndicate Underwriting Cartel reported an alarming rise in losses in the space salvage industry. Cartel spokesman Ludwig Tanaka released statistics for the last twelve months about the most perilous of human occupations at the Underwriting Cartel's headquarters in New Rome.

Long considered one of the deadliest professions, space salvage recently eclipsed both asteroid mining and the Bering Sea fishing trade in claims per policy.

Tanaka pointedly warned the salvage industry that it must improve operations to reduce claims from damaged equipment, injuries and loss of life. The Cartel may soon require all salvage operators to replace high-risk employees such as Retrieval Specialists and Wreckage Wranglers with expendable slaves and serfs. Since the Cartel does not offer insurance for unpaid workers, their loss would not warrant compensation.

Outside of the headquarters, a noisy and begrimed group of Enlightenment Crusaders rallied in support of slave and serf rights. Many of the Crusader crackpots demanded that servitude and slavery be abolished in EurAfrica as was done long ago in Free City.

New Roman police dispersed the protesters at 3 PM without incident.

19. The subtlety
of the moment

It was just past 6 AM.

Ryo trudged down the long hallway towards his
apartment.

Lieutenant Zmuda and the Coroner's Assistant
had dropped him off in front of his building in
the Ballaghaderreen District of Free City and
now the bleary Investigator just wanted to get a
few hours of sleep.

As Ryo fumbled with the lock he realized that at
least *he* could take the morning off and recover.
The equally hardworking Zmuda had planned to
turn over Nate Briggs' body to the Special
Investigations Pathologist and then dash over to
Free City University for a long day's labor as
Professor Malcolm Evans.

Ryo pushed open the door.

The flickery overhead light in his minuscule
kitchen was on. He frowned at the anomaly. Had
he left it lit when he departed three days ago?

A short and full-figured young woman wrapped
in a yellow terry cloth bathrobe with a half-
dozen long braidings of honey-brown hair smiled

124

at him from the stove.

Was he dreaming or perhaps in the wrong apartment?

He stared dumbly at the winsome cook. Who was she?

"Oh good, you're back," the woman said. "Your wee tyke will be so happy to see you before she sets off for school."

Ryo nodded with long-delayed recognition; it was Sabra MacFarland, Dilma's new nanny.

• • •

Unfortunately, Jasper realized with some exasperation, he had no idea of where Lieutenant Zmuda was just now. He glanced at the message that Mixion had just decoded from the contact in Tunis. The Lieutenant would certainly want to study it as soon as possible; but where was he?

Unlike Mixion who seemed to know with almost spooky accuracy where their elusive boss was at any particular time, the big Australian often struggled for hours to find him.

Zmuda *rarely* answered his communication device and often didn't even carry the unit with him.

Torn From On High

He frequently neglected to tell his CRAMP sidekicks about his plans for the day, and if he did, he seldom followed his own agenda.

Jasper passed a few students in the 12th floor hallway on their way to early morning classes.

The big man produced a ring of keys and let himself into the little faculty office that Zmuda sometimes used as Professor Malcolm Evans.

The cramped room was piled high with scientific journals, long-lost student papers, misplaced biology projects and a disturbing number of abandoned coffee cups; but no Zmuda.

Jasper rolled his eyes at the messy workroom before locking the door. Perhaps the head spy was in the basement lab or maybe at the Student Union.

• • •

Nearly four hundred thousand kilometers away, it was well past midnight in the sleazy bar at the Tycho Crater Outpost on the Moon.

"HAH!" Rollo scoffed at the tall tale "You are *such* a lying bastard!"

Bowie leered a bit at his bar mate before downing his fourth shot of Serengeti whiskey. "Alright, you friggin' caught me."

Schleim and Wolfe both burst into laughter.

Rollo beamed at his drunken pals, "So how *did* you kill that thieving low-life?"

Bowie glanced around the crowded tavern before answering, "I shot him in the neck with my bad-assed new weapon. Wolfe's got one too." He smiled menacingly, "It makes a tiny hole on one side and a fist-sized crater on the other."

Schleim squinted thickly at the others.

Rollo drunkenly poked his grimy fingertips into one of the empty shot glasses.

"It don't kill 'em," Bowie sloshed unsteadily about under the influence of the liquor, "it just makes 'em stop movin'. After that, you can do whatever you want to them."

Rollo looked like he was going to puke, "Where'd you boneheads get these guns?"

"A military jerk from Tunis. He pays us ten grand for each job." Bowie waved to the waitress for another round; "He's got a killing for old Wolfie coming up in New Rome. Maybe he'll take you along..."

"I said it before," Rollo roared in reply, "you are *such* a lying bastard!"

Torn From On High

• • •

Dilma bounded out of her bedroom attired in her pink pajamas just after Sabra had tiptoed into the girl's room to awaken her for breakfast.

The merry twelve-year-old gleefully wrapped her spindly arms around Ryo's neck and favored him with a wet and sloppy kiss on the cheek.

"Hi Daddy, welcome back!"

The bone-weary detective found it hard to resist the energetic lovefest supplied by his exuberant charge. "Good morning, kitten. I really missed you."

She stared appraisingly into his dark eyes for several seconds, "You look *so* tired!" She tilted her head a bit, "And rather worried about something, I think."

Ryo kissed her forehead, "It's just work, nothing important."

Sabra stood quietly in the background and admired how the man and the girl seemed to effortlessly bring out the best in each other.

Ryo glanced up at Sabra, "What have you two been doing with your time together?"

"Well;" Dilma started, "two days ago we walked around the district for awhile and Sabra let me

128

try on some *really* pretty clothes at *Plumage and Baubles* on Fitzroy Street."

"And how did you look?"

"Sabra said just like a Crusader," Dilma reported in earnest.

"What about yesterday?"

Sabra silently ducked back into the girl's room.

"We went to the park!" Dilma's eyes lit up, "I got my face painted like a butterfly and I ate a bunch of really good food. Have you ever had Thai/Martian food before?"

Ryo thought for a minute, "Thai/Martian, I think so. It's very spicy, right?"

The girl nodded.

Sabra reappeared with Dilma's new headband and blue-feathered boa, "Would you like to show these off to Ryo before you eat and head off to school?"

Dilma eagerly donned the treasured garb.

The threesome enjoyed a happy breakfast of pancakes together.

When Dilma finished up, Ryo sent the girl off to

change into her school clothes.

As Sabra scooped the last of the pancakes from her plate, she grinned at the reinvigorated man, "She really adores you."

"And you, as well," he returned her smile.

"She wanted me to ask you," Sabra ventured, "if it would be alright if I bought her some new clothes?"

"Certainly, would a hundred Units cover the cost?"

"That will be more than enough, thank you," Sabra nodded. "Would a few Enlightenment Crusade outfits be alright?"

"Of course."

"Great, she'll be so happy about that," the woman reported.

Ryo's face darkened, "I afraid that I'll have to travel more than I thought for a few weeks. Will you be able to look after Dilma while I'm away?"

Sabra felt a surprising surge of excitement at the question, "I'd *love* to."

• • •

He'd been searching around the University for Zmuda for nearly two hours.

As Jasper strolled past the 3rd floor Lecture Hall, he suddenly heard the booming disembodied voice of the missing man.

"...as you can see in the image on the screen...Chlorarachniophyte algae contains two distinctly different nuclei."

Jasper stopped and peeked into the crowded hall. There at the lectern was the Lieutenant in his day job as a Biology professor.

Zmuda continued, *"Your assignment for next week will be to read chapters 20 through 24. I will greatly favor anyone who mentions other cells that contain multiple nuclei during the Monday class."*

The professor gathered up his papers.

A throng of departing students filed past Jasper. He pressed his way into the exiting mob and approached the lectern.

An attractive young woman queried the haggard professor about a missed assignment.

Jasper waited quietly for the student to finish.

The woman wandered off a few minutes later

131

and the two men were alone in the lecture hall.

"Professor;" Jasper produced the sheet of paper that Mixion had given him earlier in the CRAMP office, "you might be interested in this."

After several seconds of dogged study, Zmuda scowled at the string of numbers and letters, "What does it mean?"

Jasper grinned at his befuddled boss, "It's an ancient coordinates system used in twenty-first century maps."

The Lieutenant's shoulders sagged, "I'm too tired for games, Jasper."

"I'm sure you'll like this one," the burly Australian laughed, "it's the precise location of some remote ruins in the Saharan Desert inexplicably guarded by two men with guns. Our pal in Tunis thought that you could use this information."

"OH!" Zmuda stared at the note with sudden interest, "Alright then, let's get back to the office and see what we can uncover about this place."

20. The night demon

"WAKE *UP* OLD MAN!"

Seamus gasped under the crushing pressure on his chest.

"I'll *friggin'* kill you if I don't get answers!" the husky young goon growled.

Seamus's thin old ribs were fracturing one by one under the weight; if one should pierce his lungs, he would bleed to death in short order. The old man warily opened his eyes. "Wha...what...do you want?" he gasped.

The punk backhanded Seamus's craggy face, which caused the old man to briefly black out.

"No...more..," Seamus finally rasped, "I'll...talk."

The thug lifted his knee from the old man's chest. "I knew you would, you bastard!"

Seamus struggled to catch his breath.

"What the hell where you doing on the *Billikin*?" the mysterious assailant sneered as he withdrew a long and slender knife from the sheath on this belt.

"I...haven't been on...the ship for years."

Torn From On High

"Lies!"

The thug slowly lowered the razor sharp tip of the weapon towards Seamus's face.

The old man cringed, "The Inquisitor's Office...they told me I had to go. They needed someone to identify the bodies."

The goon swung around and pounded the tip of the dagger into the top of the nightstand. "You talked too much to the News people, old man!"

"I..," the trauma of the late night attack caused Seamus's head to spin, "...they were my friends."

The attacker pulled the knife free and ever-so-slowly slid the tip towards the old man's throat, "Who are they looking for?"

"I don't know," Seamus whimpered, "they don't have any suspects."

"That's *not* what I heard," the thug flicked the tip back and nicked the old man's chin.

Seamus was now quite certain that the punk would kill him.

A curious and rather soft squeaking sound caught the attention of both the old man and the young criminal. It was a common sound that people hear with such regularity that most ignore it. The barely audible noise was that of a door hinge in need of oil as it slowly opened.

Both men turned towards the closet door.

A sinister purple flash and crackling retort filled the tiny bedroom.

The attacker stiffened and briefly convulsed in wide-eyed terror. He lurched heavily to the floor and twitched several times.

"Are you alright?" the almost angelic voice of a young woman cut through the eerie blue haze that smelled of singed flesh. A petite redhead stepped over the glassy-eyed punk and stood next to the badly injured old man. She was still clutched the General Issue Police Stunner that had put an end to the assault.

"Yes;" he gasped, "who...are you?"

She smiled coyly, "A friend who was sent to guard over you." The mysterious woman's fingertips glided lightly over Seamus's craggy face.

"Thank you," he whispered.

"Certainly, sweetie." She turned and spitefully kicked the crumbled thug in the ribs.

"Ah crap! It seems that I may have used a bit too

much force in the process." The woman prodded the motionless attacker with the tip of her black knee-high boot, "Unfortunately I killed the punk."

• • •

Twenty minutes later Ryo and Lieutenant Zmuda stood over the carcass.

"Sorry Boss," the woman apologized.

"Well;" Zmuda snapped with frustration, "I wish that you'd been more careful."

"Twenty-fifth century Police weapons are fairly new to me," the redhead grimaced.

"At least Seamus survived," Ryo noted as he studied the singed corpse of the punk.

The woman knelt over the dead man and twisted the head of the slowly stiffening body, "Any idea of who this goon is?"

"No," Ryo replied, "we can run his DNA through the Crime Lab Database but we don't always get a match. Meanwhile Seamus is still in danger until we can find out who sent this guy over here to rough him up."

Seamus followed the discussion with dismay.

"What if," Zmuda bit his lip, "we stage this to look like a double murder?"

Ryo stroked his stubbly chin, "That would take Seamus out of the picture and give us some time to figure out more about our dead friend."

Zmuda and the woman both nodded.

While Ryo contacted the Coroner's Office for yet another late night pickup, the Lieutenant summoned Mixion from the CRAMP office with a satchel of medical supplies.

When she arrived, Zmuda readied a syringe filled with a pale yellow fluid.

Seamus stared warily at the Lieutenant, "What is that?"

Zmuda twitched a bit as he injected the substance into the old man's thin arm, "It's a particularly strong sedative that will make it seem as if you are dead. We'll make a big show when we haul you out of here and everyone will assume that you were killed during a burglary."

Seamus's eyes fluttered, "What happens...next?"

The Lieutenant withdrew the needle, "You will wake up in a better place."

21. News Item: Elderly gent attacked in apartment

Dateline: 7th of September, 2446; Free City, Earth

Free City Police are at a loss to explain the brutal murder of a reclusive ninety-seven year-old retired spacecraft crewman at his apartment in the tranquil Eire District of the fair city.

Neighbors summoned the police late last night to check on a violent altercation of some sort in the man's apartment. When the officers entered the residence they discovered two bodies, those of the victim and the assailant.

Coroner's Officials removed both corpses early this morning and the Inquisitor's Office has sealed the crime scene pending further investigation.

Neither a motive for the unprecedented attack nor the names of the dead have been released by investigators. Building tenants revealed that the anonymous elderly gentleman kept to himself and may have confronted a burglar rummaging around in the apartment. Speculation suggests that the old man managed to mortally wound his attacker before succumbing himself.

The two deaths mark only the fourth and fifth homicides in the staid Eire District this year.

22. Ominous

"What the *hell* happened to Slime?" Bowie slammed his fist on the bar, which caused the accumulation of empty shot glasses to clatter and quake.

The bartender warily watched the befouled threesome from the other end of the bar.

Wolfe nodded, "How does a badass roughneck like Slime get killed by a spindly old geezer?"

Rollo stared drunkenly at the two big Goons.

"I want to know everything that you two idiots found out in Free City. Wolfie, you saw the bodies in the morgue;" Bowie absent-mindedly picked at a soiled napkin, "what do you think happened?"

"Ah; let me see," Wolfe rubbed his bloodshot eyes as he thought, "the old man had a cut on his chin and a lot of bruises. Slime had a big black burn on his chest."

"There's something's strange about all of this;" Bowie glowered, "it sounds like Slime got hit with a Stunner. Why would the old man have a police weapon?"

Wolfe shrugged.

Bowie stared at the bartender and tapped his finger several times on the bar. The barman nodded nervously and quickly brought over another round for the well-oiled trio.

"Rollo, what happened to the old man's body?" the head Goon asked.

"They buried him at Old Saint Mary's," Rollo grinned, "I watched the whole thing with a couple of the grave diggers."

"What about Slime?" Wolfe wondered as he downed his drink "Nobody's claimed his body."

"Leave him to rot at the morgue!" Bowie fumed. "It's what he deserves for getting killed by an old walking bag of bones!"

"I guess that you're right," Wolfe said. "Well;" he patted at the bulge underneath his black jacket, "I've got a job to do." He grabbed Rollo's collar as he stood up, "Come on dumby; you're in on this one."

• • •

He seemed to be coming around, Mixion noted.

Seamus's craggy old face slowly rippled as he lay stretched out on the cot in the CRAMP situation room.

Torn From On High

Jasper and the Lieutenant had hauled the unconscious gent from the Free City Morgue to the secret workroom two days ago packed gently away in a stout shipping crate conspicuously marked 'FRAGILE! -- Cytoplasm Scanning Apparatus -- THIS SIDE UP!'

As his alter ego, Biology Professor Malcolm Evans, Zmuda planned to make a big show of sending the now empty crate away in a few days, claiming that the supposed scanner that it contained was not up to par.

Seamus's eyes fluttered and finally opened.

He gasped a bit and stared at the woman.

"Where...where am I?"

"Safe, I assure you," she smiled.

He nodded sleepily.

Nearly an hour later, Mixion had gotten the old spaceman to sit up on the edge of the cot. He clutched a water-filled mug with a spill-proof lid that he sampled every few minutes.

"How long has it been, my dear?"

"Oh, let's see;" she started, "you were attacked in the apartment about a week ago. We left you in conspicuous view at the Morgue for a day on a specially heated gurney behind the big windows in one of the Examining Rooms. Jasper kept a close watch over you during that ghoulish exhibition."

Seamus frowned, "Why did you do that, child?"

"It wasn't my idea, but it makes sense," she told him. "We are trying to track down whoever it is that sent the thug to rough you up. Inspector Trop still thinks that a girl friend or ex-wife may show up to claim the body of the dead punk. Having your old carcass out in plain sight adds to the fiction of your death that we planted in the news. Another possibility is that a colleague of the mysterious dead burglar was one of the forty-seven people who happened to stroll by the Examining Room while you were there. He or she would probably report back that you were, in fact, dead."

The old man followed along with a look of consternation.

"Ryo Trop and a few plainclothes Inspectors attended a funeral where an empty casket supposedly containing your remains was buried at the Old Saint Mary's Cemetery." She grinned mischievously, "He said that it was quite touching."

"That sounds like much more of an honor than an old curmudgeon like me deserves."

Seamus sipped some water, "What happens now?"

She dithered at the question, "I don't know. You can stay here for a little while. We can't risk settling you elsewhere in Free City or really anywhere in neighboring EurAfrica for fear that someone might spot you. Eventually, we'll have to move you to a safe location."

"I suppose you're right," he sighed.

• • •

Wolfe was already regretting taking Rollo along on such an important job. It was true that he was one of the Goons now but he was just *so* damn stupid.

"Come on, you idiot!" the heavyset punk barked.

They bumped their way down the crowded New Roman sidewalk towards the nightclub.

"What's the hurry, Wolfie?"

The big man spun around and stared angrily at the underling, "If we pull this off then we'll split up ten thousand Units."

Rollo grinned doltishly, "Oh yeah."

The two punks pushed past a noisy group of Enlightenment Crusaders clustered around the
144

entrance to the EurAfrican Imperial Bank.

"Wolfie? I got one question."

"What now?" he growled impatiently.

"Who *is* this guy that we're supposed to kill?"

Wolfe perfunctorily pointed to the *Hissing Serpent* nightclub. "I don't know who he is or what he looks like."

Rollo stared dimly at his husky cohort, "How the hell are we gonna kill him if we don't know who he is?"

"A Liaison Agent named Macaroni or Macgillicutty, something like that, is going to introduce us to a spy from Free City."

"Why?"

"It was set up weeks ago by the military, you idiot. Agent Macaroni thinks we have some new information to pass along to the Free City busybodies."

Rollo seemed to barely comprehend what was about to happen, "We gonna kill everybody?"

A menacing sneer darted across Wolfe's face, "We just need to get the spy. Anyone who dies after that counts as good luck."

Torn From On High

●●●

As she often did late in the day on Mondays, Keira Norton was frittering away a few stray hours of the workweek by thumbing through the Free City Liaison Office Message Postings.

The hundred or so notations and intra-agency requests represented a fascinating view of what was transpiring just beyond the hubbub and noise of everyday life in Free City and the Fiefdoms.

The habit had started a little over a year ago when Keira had come upon an appeal in the Message Postings by the Free City Consular in Dublin for some help in securing a few new household staff members. The work had been easy and had, by lucky chance, led to an exciting months-long adventure dashing across the Solar System with the highly esteemed Inspector Ryo Trop in search of pirates and stolen antimatter.

Keira grinned as she recalled that she had met Lev Fesai during that escapade.

Most of today's listings were routine: a request for a Liaison Agent to help settle a group of fifteen new arrivals to Free City from IndoPacifica, a query about how to negotiate prices for bulk tea leaves in East Africa and a plea for a guest lecturer in International Affairs at the University of Buenos Aires.

146

But Item 87 had caught her attention for some reason. An unnamed department at Free City University was seeking help to discreetly relocate a mysterious elderly gentleman. Details were maddeningly missing from the notice. Was it perhaps an old professor who'd gone embarrassingly bonkers and now had to be quietly shuffled away to avoid a scandal? Or was it something else?

She reread the notice several times, trying in vain to parse more meaning than was possible from the dozen and a half words.

Finally on a whim, Keira entered her Liaison Office ID number at the bottom of the notice and pressed 'Enter.' She had now officially expressed a desire to take on Item 87 in the current Free City Liaison Office Message Postings.

• • •

"I'm sorry to say that I don't care much for this particular city," Ryo shook his head in disdain.

"Really?" The Lieutenant was taken aback by the declaration, "I rather like New Rome."

The two old friends strolled together towards a rather seedy looking nightspot called *The Hissing Serpent*.

"New Rome seems too self-absorbed and mean-

147

spirited compared to the generally jovial atmosphere of Free City."

"I guess that much is true," Zmuda laughed, "at least it's better than Dublin or Tunis."

"What's wrong with Dublin?" Ryo chortled.

"Nothing, nothing," Zmuda smiled.

The cop and the spy made their way into the garish drinking establishment.

• • •

"Hi, sugar. How's the deciphering going?" Jasper leaned down and kissed Mixion's cheek as she labored away with the latest message from Tunis.

She flashed a huge grin at the affectionate greeting.

The two junior spies had slowly become much more than mere coworkers.

Mixion glanced down at the several sheets of paper spread out on the desk, "I'm just starting, but it looks like it should be an easy decryption."

He stared over her shoulders as she worked.

"Well; that's odd," Mixion tapped at the character that she'd just written.

"An exclamation point?" Jasper noted.

"Yes. Our guy in Tunis has never used one before." She added a seven and a one to the message, "Jasp; take a look in the appendix of the Morse Code book and find out if exclamation points have any special meanings."

He nodded pleasantly.

She scribed out several more characters while the big man thumbed through the reference.

"Big surprise," he finally chortled, "exclamation means urgent."

"Mmm," Mixion finished up with the decoding. "OK; I have !719RNZTLLLIK."

Jasper tilted his head as he studied the string of numbers and letters, "I guess it is important, whatever it is."

"Nothing pops out," she noted. "Perhaps it's reversed. He's been doing that a lot lately."

"That makes sense," Jasper noted, "exclamation points usually go at the end of sentences."

She inverted the string, which yielded 'KILLLTZNR917!'

Jasper pointed to the characters, "Three 'Ls?' That's strange."

"WAIT!" Mixion held up her hand to stop him.

She hastily wrote out 'KILL-LT-Z'

"Kill Lieutenant Z? 'Z' *must* mean Zmuda."

Mixion quivered as she continued, "N-R? New Rome?"

"AH, CRIPES!" Jasper shouted. "9-17 is today!"

"Kill Lieutenant Zmuda, New Rome 9-17!" She dropped the pencil and stared up at him, "We've got to do something!"

The burly Australian was uncharacteristically silent.

"What about his communication device?" Jasper finally asked.

The woman slid open the desk drawer with a look of utter horror, "It's here! The boss forgot to take it with him."

"OK; he's with Ryo Trop, right?"

Mixion nodded.

"Let's just get a hold of him."

She hurriedly tapped out his number.

'Delivery denied at New Roman Message Nexus - - Issuer of Block: UNAVAILABLE,' flashed on the communication screen.

Mixion leapt to her feet, "WHO ELSE IS IN NEW ROME?"

Jasper studied the short roster of trusted operatives, "It doesn't look good..."

"Damn it!" She stared at the list of names, "What about her?"

"No;" Jasper shook his head in dread, "the New Roman police locked her up last night for drunk and disorderly conduct. She'll be in jail until next week."

Mixion nervously dug her nails into Jasper's arm as she studied the other names.

"There! Contact this guy!"

Jasper quickly tapped out an imperative message to the improbable savior, "Hopefully it will work, he's not a regular."

23. *The Hissing Serpent*

"There's Mac!" Ryo pointed to the third booth to
the left in the dim and musty back section of *The
Hissing Serpent* nightclub.

Liaison Agent Hugo Mackillroy waved to the old
Inspector. Ryo nudged the Lieutenant towards
the table.

"Wait a minute," Zmuda resisted. "Do you
recognize the two bruisers with him?"

"No;" Ryo shook his head, "but if they are OK
with Mac, they're OK with me."

"I have a weird feeling about those two," the
Lieutenant muttered.

"Me too," Ryo frowned. "Good, bad or ugly,
we're here to collect some leads for our stalled
investigations."

Zmuda donned a wide smile, "I suppose you're
right."

"Mac! It's good to see you again," Ryo reached
across the table bestrewn with empty drink
glasses to offer a hand to his old pal.

"It's been a long time," the Liaison Agent
pumped Ryo's arm with vigor. "This is Mr.

Wolfe and his colleague, Mr. Rollo."

"Gentleman;" the old Investigator bowed slightly, "this is...uh..."

"Uloff Lebrinski," Zmuda grinned.

"Lebrinski, are you the Free City spy that Agent Macaroni promised us?"

"Mackillroy," Ryo corrected Wolfe, "Agent Hugo Mackillroy."

"You're Trop. We know all about you" Wolfe sneered a bit. "Ryo Trop, age 55, Inspector Second Class with the Free City Inquisitor's Office. ID number 783682. Divorced with one young kid. Your home is at Number 17, Na Daracha Ársa Street, Apartment 392, in the Ballaghaderreen District of Free City."

"There's just one thing that you've gotten wrong, Mr. Wolfe."

"What's that?" the big man smirked.

It was a rather rough and tumble effort at verbal intimidation, Ryo decided, a game that he could play quite well. He let the young punk hang for several seconds as he stroked his chin.

"I was recently upgraded to Inspector First Class."

153

Wolfe burst into laughter, "Fair enough, old man!"

The rather inebriated Rollo cackled along with Wolfe.

Ryo could sense an odd underlying tow of duplicity in the young men.

"Yes;" Zmuda finally answered in an effort to ease some of the tension at the booth, "I have some connection to a spy organization in Free City."

"Excellent! Have a seat," Wolfe grinned. "Bevvies for the table on me!"

• • •

They were well into their fourth round of drinks with no end in sight when Ryo spotted a familiar face at the bar.

The old Investigator had steadfastly stuck to his habit of imbibing in only a single beverage during the course of a gathering. At this point he was certainly the only one at the booth still in full possession of his wits.

Mac, Zmuda and the two roughnecks merrily quaffed the latest offerings as the waitress deposited them on the table.

While the others roared at a rather crude joke involving a randy barmaid, Ryo studied the tall slim man in his mid-twenties who stared at him from the bar.

The fellow unobtrusively beckoned to him.

Ryo discreetly nodded in reply.

"Gentleman," the old Investigator started, "I'll check with the bartender to see if he's got a certain rare old Irish Whiskey that will knock you into the next county."

"Here, here!" Mac offered a toast with his now empty tumbler.

Ryo slipped out of the booth and theatrically staggered off.

The smutty jokes began anew.

The Investigator picked a spot at the bar just to the left of the man and well away from the bartender. He wanted as much time as possible to find out what was happening before he had to continue his ruse regarding ancient spirits.

"Lev; what are you doing here?" Ryo whispered.

The young man glanced back at the raucous group at the booth, "I'm so glad I found you. Mixion sent me."

Ryo stretched lethargically to cover his growing concern, "Really? What's up?"

"Take a look," Lev produced his communication device and casually set it on the bar between them.

Ryo picked up a soiled bar napkin and dabbed at his lips as he read the display screen out of the corner of his eye.

'Plot to kill Lt. Z in New Rome today!
INTERCEPT & PROTECT AT ALL COSTS!'

"Son of a...," Ryo turned and waved amiably to the soused group at the booth, "I *thought* that there was something sketchy about this meeting." The Investigator swiveled around and glowered for several seconds. "Any idea as to how I could tip off Zmuda without the others knowing?" he whispered.

Lev tapped several times at the communication device screen and a second message appeared from Mixion.

'Make reference to Z's wife Charlotte when intercepting.'

Ryo flagged down the barman. "That makes sense."

"I don't understand," Lev whispered.
156

The bartender ambled towards them.

"Zmuda has never been married." The older man stared at his young friend for just an instant, "When all hell breaks loose, get the Lieutenant out of here no matter what. Don't worry about me or anyone else."

"OK."

The bartender smiled at Ryo, "What'll it be, my friend?"

Ryo beamed wickedly at the question, "We've got a bet going on in the booth over there that the big guy dressed in black can't drink a shot of pure grain alcohol without vomiting."

The barman snorted at the wager, "I'll put ten Units on barfing!"

"You got it," Ryo laughed. "What do you have that'll do the job?"

"OH; you want *Dragon's Breath Black Rum* from Indonesia. It's about as puke-inducing as you can get."

"Perfect. Give me a large tumbler full."

The bartender retrieved a stout black bottle labeled with a stylized skull and crossbones, "Enjoy!"

Ryo tapped out the payment and added a huge
tip for the man. He was, after all, probably not
going to collect on his bet.

The Investigator lumbered back to the booth
with the vile black liquid and carefully studied
the arrangement of the others around the table.
He had only an unlikely chance of successfully
saving himself and the Lieutenant.

The bench curved in a semicircle around the
back of the table; fortunately Zmuda was at one
end and could easily dash away. Ryo's spot was
at the opposite end, which was equally
advantageous. But Mac was right in the middle,
sandwiched tightly between Rollo and Wolfe.

Ryo winced when he realized that the Liaison
Agent could not escape unscathed.

"AH, he's back!" bellowed Mac.

Ryo slipped into the booth next to Wolfe and
placed his palm protectively over the tumbler
filled with nearly pure grain alcohol.

"Alright;" harangued Wolfe, "who's got the balls
to take the first shot?"

The old Investigator slowly nodded and stared
across the table at Zmuda. He produced a wide,
friendly grin when he was sure that the spy was

paying attention to him. "Well; it won't be him," Ryo joked.

"Why not?" Rollo asked.

Ryo's outwardly calm appearance belied his extreme inner anxiety.

Zmuda tipped his head and frowned, he now seemed well aware that something was amiss.

"His dear wife Charlotte will kill him if she finds out that he's been drinking."

Uproarious laughter erupted at the table.

Zmuda's eyes grew huge at the quip, he knew.

While their intoxicated tablemates harassed and belittled the Lieutenant, Ryo's eyes leapt towards the bar where Lev was waiting.

The young man quickly pointed one finger at the side exit.

Zmuda nodded with a grim look of acknowledgment and eased himself up to depart.

"HEY!" Wolfe produced a small and very unusual handgun, "Where the HELL are you going?"

Zmuda stopped, "You guys are asses. I need

some air."

"Sit down, you bastard!" Wolfe pointed the gun at the man; "We know that you ordered the murder of Madame Sophia Kufuzu last year. Now it's your turn to die."

The nightclub grew eerily quiet.

Ryo let his hand slip off the top of the tumbler.

CRASH! A porcelain plate shattered on the floor.

Wolfe turned towards the sound of the disturbance.

Ryo used the diversion to fling the contents of the tumbler into the big Goon's eyes.

Wolfe screeched in agony.

Ryo slammed the man's pistol hand onto the tabletop and the gun skittered across the floor.

Lev dashed over and he and Zmuda sprinted away.

Mac had a look of utter terror as he realized that he was unable to escape the unfolding disaster.

Ryo quickly backed away from the table, glancing around as he moved, trying in vain to
160

spot the missing side arm: it was likely one of the particle beam weapons that had done in Nate Briggs and Captain Takahashi.

Lev pried open the exit door and he and Zmuda waited for just an instant as Ryo trotted their way.

"The grenade!" yelped Wolfe, "GET THEM WITH THE FRIGGIN' GRENADE!"

Rollo hastily retrieved a fragmentation grenade from his jacket and pulled the pin.

The dimwitted punk hesitated as the spy, the cop and the scruffy young man stood at the exit.

With the vile black liquid running down his face, Wolfe clawed madly at his burning eyes.

Rollo had a pathetic look of uncertainty; "It's a ten second delay, right?"

"NO FIVE, YOU IDIOT!" screamed Wolfe.

The grenade exploded in Rollo's chubby right hand just as his arm arched above his head for the unfortunately postponed pitch.

The concussive force of the blast and the frightfully high number of razor sharp bits of metal shrapnel instantly killed Liaison Agent Hugo Mackillroy and the two thugs.

24. News Item: Nightclub damaged by explosion

Dateline: 18th of September, 2446; New Rome, Earth

"We've had drunken altercations at the *Hissing Serpent* before," reported blood-splattered Bartender Jackson Ito, "but never anything like that."

New Roman police are currently struggling to explain why an apparently friendly gathering involving three unidentified Free City residents and two mysterious locals suddenly went wrong last night at the nightspot on Spinoza Street.

Early reports indicate that three people were killed.

Dozens of drunken patrons were injured, some quite seriously, when a scuffle apparently broke out in a back booth.

Several barflies reported that a wager involving drinking prowess seemed to have gone wrong which prompted one of the dead men to draw a sidearm and a second combatant to respond with a military-grade fragmentation grenade. The ensuing blast killed both men.

An apparently innocent Free City resident was also killed.

Due to the still murky details and the death of a Free City citizen, the New Roman authorities have asked the Free City Inquisitor's Office to aid with the perplexing case.

The *Hissing Serpent* will be closed for at least a week to allow for repairs.

25. The aftermath of the blast

Fortunately the crime scene was nearly devoid of others at this early hour.

"Here you go Inspector," the young New Roman crime scene technician uncovered the last of the three corpses that were scattered around the ruins of the back booth at the *Hissing Serpent*.

Ryo winced as he bent over to look at the body. He still had four or five tiny shards of metal trapped annoyingly just under the skin of his back.

But the sight of this particular body was much more painful than the stray bits of shrapnel: It was the badly mangled remains of his old friend Mac.

The naive assistant was obviously unaware of the older man's distress.

Cops and Liaison Agents died in the line of duty all of the time, but Ryo had been pals with Mac for decades.

The old investigator turned to the novice technician, "Any idea of who he is?"

The kid shook his head, "No sir. All we know for sure is that he's from Free City."

164

"Alright, crate him up. The Consular's people will ship him straight away to our Morgue and we will let you know what we find out."

The old investigator was quite eager to get Mac's body safely away from the prying eyes of the hapless New Roman and EurAfrican officials. If they stumbled upon the fact that Mac was a Free City Liaison Agent then both Ryo's investigation into the assault on Seamus and the murders onboard the *Billikin* and the Lieutenant's efforts to unravel the desert mystery would be compromised.

"Yes sir," the young man chirped, "I'll get right on it."

Zmuda returned to the shattered rear section of the bar. He'd been introduced earlier to the few New Roman cops loitering around the crime scene as Ryo's coworker, Inspector Third Class Hal Zelichowska.

It had been a long and harrowing night for both men.

Lev had managed to spirit the cop and the spy away just after the altercation and clean them up in a room at a local boardinghouse used mainly by Enlightenment Crusaders. Ryo had hastily called Chief Inspector Helga Bennet in Free City and detailed the ill-fated meeting. Helga was adamant that they *must* continue the dual investigations and recover Mac's body at once with a minimum of fuss.

Ryo and Zmuda both reluctantly agreed.

They now had to determine how the thugs knew of Zmuda's involvement in the assassination of Madame Kufuzu a year earlier.

As Inspector Third Class Hal Zelichowska, the Lieutenant bowed a bit in deference to Ryo, "Well boss, we have the names of the two other victims."

"Do tell."

"The knucklehead with the Frag grenade was Norman Rollo, a petty punk most recently from Mariner's Station on Mars. Nobody seems to know where he got the advanced munitions."

Ryo stroked his chin in thought, "What about the other guy?"

"Fritzi Wolfe, an up and coming hoodlum apparently from Nairobi who has recently had several very large and unexplained payments made to his personal account. Both men have affiliations with a small gang called the 'Goons' that engages in intimidation and murder for hire."

"Well; that's a bit of a break."
166

After some reflection, Ryo continued, "What about the gun?"

Zmuda glanced around the nearly deserted bar.

The Lieutenant opened his coat to reveal the unusual weapon; "I spotted it under one of the booths at the front of the bar. I grabbed it while you and the New Roman cop where looking at the bodies."

Ryo smiled to his pal.

"I'd like to get it back to the CRAMP lab as soon as possible," Zmuda whispered.

"Good idea. Slip out with it now, I'll cover for you."

Zmuda seemed reluctant to leave, "What about you?"

Ryo groaned from the emotional and physical battering of the last twelve hours, "I'm going to take a quick trip to Nairobi to see what I can find out about Mr. Fritzi Wolfe."

• • •

Bowie swaggered unannounced into the office at the EurAfrican Imperial Military Base in Tunis and laid his gun on the cluttered desk, "I need another one of these gems."

167

Torn From On High

Commander Frédéric Rameau growled as he looked up from his paperwork, "Turn in your Entrance Authorization, I don't want you to come around here again."

"Why the hell not?" Bowie asked with some annoyance.

The Head of Covert Operations took his time before he answered; he was, after all, in charge of the various dirty deeds that the Goons had been paid to accomplish. Rameau leisurely replaced the thug's nearly depleted Particle Beam weapon with a freshly charged weapon that he retrieved from his gun cabinet.

"First; a cheap punk like you shouldn't be on an elite military base. I can't have you parading around here like an arrogant peacock. You had your chance years ago but you just couldn't handle Paramilitary training. Second; there can be no visible connection between your band of half-wit hoodlums and the honorable Empire of EurAfrica."

"I quit the Paramilitarists because of hard asses like you," Bowie laughed at the ramrod Commander. "We both know that what I do ain't cheap and that there's no such thing as honor in EurAfrica."

"Perhaps not;" Rameau shot back, "but your idiot cohorts *did* manage to screw up the

168

assassination that the Kufuzu family ordered. That opportunity may never present itself again."

"I shouldn't have let Wolfe take Rollo with him;" the big Goon winced, "he was such a moron."

The Commander's face hardened, "How you accomplish the tasks that you're paid to do does not concern me. What I require is that you actually succeed in doing them."

Bowie stood in terse silence while Rameau scribbled some instructions on a sheet of paper.

"To appease the Kufuzu family after your recent screw up, I want you kill this man. My sources indicate that he mucked up the assassination attempt." The Commander handed him a thick dossier entitled *Ryo Trop, Free City Inquisitor's Office*.

The burly hired hand studied the file and stared at one of the many photographs, "He's got a cute family; perhaps I'll mow down the whole group."

The Commander nodded curtly, "That would be a nice touch."

• • •

Far to the southwest, the weary old Inspector awaited the arrival of his counterpart for the hastily arranged meeting. It was early spring in

Nairobi, Ryo observed as he sat straight-backed in the open-air cafe to avoid irritating his recent wounds.

Down the street an ancient African man tended to the nearest of a dozen or so small trees that lined this side of Kenyatta Avenue. The wrinkled skinned chap produced an obviously homemade machete fabricated from a long, sharpened scrap of charcoal-black steel flat stock with a shred of grimy old leather wrapped around one end to serve as a handle.

With well-practiced flicks, the maintenance man used the razor-edged tip to deftly trim several small branches from the tree.

When he had amassed a good-sized pile of sticks and twigs, the old fellow retrieved a long piece of heavy twine from his pocket and methodically bundled up the debris. He hoisted the tidy package of limbs and trudged off to the next tree to begin the slow process again.

"Ryo?"

The old investigator twisted painfully around towards the source of the query.

It was Inspector Second Class Zara Kamchatka.

She stared at him in dismay for several seconds, "You look like crap."

170

Ryo winced as he stood to greet her, "I was a little too close to a Frag grenade that exploded in New Rome last night."

"At that sleazy bar that Mac likes?" the willowy woman sat down at the table. "I read this morning that there was some sort of drunken skirmish there."

Ryo gingerly lowered himself into his chair, "It was far worst than that, I'm afraid. Liaison Agent Hugo Mackillroy was killed along with a couple of others."

"Mac?" Zara's face darkened into a gray mask of dread.

"I'm afraid so."

After a few minutes of silence, he continued, "A CRAMP agent and I were conducting an Edict 343 investigation."

The woman's eyes grew huge at the mention of the secret operation.

"Zara; we were set up for assassination."

She trembled at the sudden wave of horrifying news. "Alright;" she whispered, "I'll do whatever I can to help out."

Ryo studied her for several seconds, she was

171

tough and wilily with a no-nonsense personality to match. Something about her had inexplicably changed in the last few minutes.

He had assumed for many years that Zara would eventually replace Helga Bennet as Chief Inspector when his cranky old boss finally retired or succumbed to the endless demands of the relentless job.

Now he wasn't so sure.

"I have two questions;" he intoned, "What do you know of a local bruiser named Fritzi Wolfe and his sidekick Norman Rollo? And do you have any information about a gang called the Goons?"

"I, uh, well..," Zara had an uncommon look of remorse. "It's not important."

"Inspector Kamchatka," Ryo growled impatiently, "thirteen people have been killed to date, all rather gruesomely. You need to tell me what you know before someone else is murdered."

Her shoulders slumped in defeat, "You're right, I screwed up.

The old Investigator glowered at his dithering coworker.

"About six months ago I was poking around in one of the slums of Nairobi for some information about the Goons. They had a small-time protection racket that was working its way into the business district and the Warlord Syndicate asked for help from the Inquisitor's Office to put an end to the scheme."

Ryo nodded.

"One night I trailed Wolfe to a pub on Moi Street and a fairly nice looking fellow struck up a conversation with me at the bar. Wolfe slipped away while I was chatting with the guy."

She pressed her hands over her eyes, "One thing led to another and after *way* too many drinks I ended up spending the night with him."

"Investigators are forbidden to engage in casual sexual relations with the locals, Inspector Kamchatka."

"I know," she whispered.

After just enough time for Zara to fret about her unforgivable misconduct, Ryo continued, "How does this all tie together?"

She glanced up repentantly at him, "The man that I slept with was Herman Bowie. I discovered about a month later that he is the top dog of the Goons."

Ryo cringed at the revelation.

"It was all a set up." Zara pressed her eyes closed, "Bowie and the other Goons knew that I was hunting around for details about their operation." Her voice cracked with shame, "Somehow Bowie managed to turn it all against me."

Ryo considered the complex ramifications of the unsavory dalliance.

Down the street, the old black man gathered up his final bundle of twigs and shuffled off.

"Wait a minute;" Ryo stared in consternation at the departing maintenance man, "you were intimate with a member of the Goons?"

Zara nodded.

"How much does this Bowie creep know of your investigation into Madame Sophia Kufuzu's death?"

She flinched at the scathing question.

"Almost everything."

26. Decisions and admonishments

"Well this is definitely it, Boss," Mixion glanced up at Lieutenant Zmuda. The poor fellow's face was pockmarked with a dozen or so tiny shrapnel wounds from the blast in New Rome.

He stared at her in disbelief, "You're sure?"

She nodded, "I have good information from two different sources. Commander Frédéric Rameau of the EurAfrican Imperial Military is definitely responsible for both the unusual particle weapons and the attack on you and Inspector Trop at the nightclub."

"Alright; I'll let Ryo know what you've discovered." He tapped his fingers on the desktop for several seconds as he contemplated the news.

"We're going to have to put a stop to these efforts by Rameau," Zmuda muttered as he turned towards the door. "I'll be back in a few hours to discuss our next move."

Mixion nodded to the Lieutenant; he almost certainly would come up with some sort of cleaver plan. "Where are you off to?" she asked.

He had an odd look of resolve as he stood at the

175

door, "I'm going down to the CRAMP lab to check over that gun that I smuggled out of the nightclub. Hopefully I can figure out some way of putting an end to this madness."

• • •

The toasted caramel smell of freshly roasted coffee beans filled the air.

Dilma stood momentarily awestruck just inside the door of the bustling *Cafe Bernardi* in the Old Town District.

A dozen paces ahead, in a thick clump of the noisy and kinetic patrons, Sabra stood next to a table of five merrily attired friends.

Dilma's hand had slipped from her nanny's a few seconds earlier when they had entered the trendy hotspot together. Now the little girl felt strangely cutoff and isolated amongst the swirling hubbub of grown-ups.

Sabra smiled flirtatiously at a handsome bearded man at the table. He blew her a kiss and winked.

The temporarily forsaken preteen at the door of the Cafe felt a nudge from behind. Dilma turned around to see what was the source of the prodding. A redheaded woman with a rather stern expression of displeasure pointed to Sabra.

"Stay with your baby-sitter, kid!" the woman growled.

The girl nodded shyly and hurried to the table.

Sabra reached down and idly stroked Dilma's braided hair as she chatted with her Enlightenment Crusade pals.

The little girl glanced timidly back towards the doorway but the mysterious woman was gone.

• • •

"Of course I'll take on the assignment," Keira grinned at Seamus. "This old relic and I have been through a lot together already."

"Excellent;" Mixion commented, "the boss is still recovering from a near-death experience in New Rome. He should be back in the office later today. I'm sure he'll approve and by the end of the week we should be able to move Seamus out of Free City for good."

The old man was visibly relieved by the news.

Keira scribbled a note to herself on a scrap of yellow paper. "I'll inform the Liaison Superintendent's Office that, until further notice, I will be attending to Item 87 in the most recent Postings."

Seamus beamed with gratitude, "Thank you, my dear."

"Mmm;" Mixion tapped her fingertips absently on her forehead as she thought, "the final nettlesome part of this whole scheme is to find a place to settle him where no one would ever think to look."

Seamus and Keira grinned at each other.

"I think we may know of just such a place," the old fellow wryly noted.

• • •

It had been going on for nearly an hour now, he realized.

"Yes, Oh Exalted One," Tariq replied as he cringed under the verbal onslaught of the tyrannical Warlord.

Daniel Kufuzu's tirade in the cool, dim cave in the isolated corner of the Sahara Desert continued unabated.

Tariq and his workmates stood in tedious tight-lipped silence while the Warlord ranted about their latest failing: The rice pudding that the madman had demanded and Qadir had spent two days procuring from a bazaar in Séguedine had been presented to him at room temperature and not chilled as he had stipulated.

EurAfrican Serfs had been raised for centuries to quietly endure the periodic scoldings of their masters, Tariq had certainly weathered many tongue-lashings in the past from Commander Frédéric Rameau; but this unending mistreatment by Kufuzu was far too extreme.

The lightly built Warlord balled up his fist and struck Qadir in the abdomen.

The stoic Serf silently winced at the punishment.

The tyrant's diatribe began anew.

Although it was not his place to question the often-absurd demands of the Warlord, Tariq was surely forming a strong dislike for the man.

• • •

"Sit down," Chief Inspector Helga Bennet said.

Ryo limped into her dim office and eased himself onto the hard wooden desk chair.

The irritable head of the Inquisitor's Office shuffled through a thick pile of papers on her desk. She pulled several sheets from the stack and handed them to Ryo.

Helga finally smiled a bit in almost a motherly way, "How are the injuries?"

Ryo nodded distractedly as he read over the reports, "Much better now that the metal shards have been removed from my thick hide."

"Since we will soon be short an Investigator," she revealed, "I need you to be in good health."

He set down the paperwork and tipped his head at her comment.

"When your investigation wraps up," Helga stared at him with her steely gray eyes, "I plan to recall Inspector Second Class Zara Kamchatka from East Africa due to her unforgivably bad judgment of late."

Ryo frowned; 'recall' meant only one thing, Zara was finished at the Inquisitor's Office.

Precluding any further discussion of the indiscretion, Helga tapped at the top sheet of Ryo's stack, "The Coroner has ruled that Nate Briggs was murdered by persons unknown. His wounds and the damage to the neck area of his spacesuit are nearly indistinguishable from those that were found on the mass murder victims onboard the *Billikin*."

"Dreadful but not unexpected," Ryo noted.

Helga smirked at his reply before continuing, "Using your recent lead regarding the misdeeds of the Goons, Inspector Heinkel down in Records has identified the deceased assailant of Mr. Seamus Nelson."

He grinned at the break in the case.

"The dead punk's name is Bertrum Hubert Schleim. He was most recently arrested in the company of Fritzi Reginald Wolfe and Herman "Bowie" Kowalski last February in Tunis for Drunk and Disorderly Conduct. They each served twelve hours and were released. You will note that on his arrest record Mr. Kowalski has some sort of military training."

Helga handed him the mugshots of the trio.

"I certainly recognize Wolfe and Schleim," Ryo noted as he studied the photos. "Now three of the four Goons are dead but I suspect that this Bowie character will be the toughest to tangle with."

"And the hardest to find," Helga added.

• • •

The Lieutenant stood at the workbench in the secret CRAMP lab and studied the internal components of the gun that he had spirited away from the crime scene in New Rome.

It was remarkably similar to the rudimentary drawings that he'd obtained from an operative in Tunis several months ago.

He gently pried aside the metal shielding to reveal the workings. Below was a tiny particle accelerator barely larger than his index finger coupled to a high-powered Rutherford Neutron generator.

Zmuda scribbled some notes about the markings on the components. Later he would attempt to track down more data about the unusual parts.

He continued to probe the interior of the little weapon.

The label on the power cell read *Matter/Antimatter Power Conversion Unit 90 volts -- 400 Kilowatt/ seconds*. It was a staggering amount of energy for such a small package.

If there was any sort of exploitable weakness in the firearm, Zmuda realized with a smile, it was surely the ultra high-powered energy source in the handgrip.

• • •

Good; Commander Frédéric Rameau thought to himself as he scrutinized the overnight commodities prices: Both titanium and aluminum futures were at an all-time high on the Warlord Syndicate Futures Market.

As he read the reports, he idly fingered the nearly depleted weapon that Bowie had left behind on his desk.

Frédéric snickered at the exorbitant numbers; his protracted efforts at intimidation were certainly paying off.

27. Anxious preparations

Ryo had spent the better part of the day hunched over one of the interface screens in the Records Room in the Inquisitor's Office basement. Most of the files that he had blearily examined contained raw data or information that was obtained through questionable means.

Due to the complex and sensitive nature of the material, it could not be accessed elsewhere.

Over many hours he had managed to track a single payoff made to Bertrum Hubert Schleim, apparently know to many as 'Slime,' back through several intermediaries to a slave merchant in Carthage Heights on the coast of North Africa.

The trail had ended there, but the merchant *had* received several large payments in the last few months from a Tunisian named Fred Bough. Through a lucky chance, Ryo had just discovered that Mr. Bough was actually Frédéric Rameau, the Commander of Covert Operations at the EurAfrican Imperial Military Base in Tunis.

Zmuda had confided earlier in the day that he had some still highly classified evidence that Commander Rameau was ultimately to blame for the many misdeeds of the Goons and that had been confirmed by Ryo's latest findings.

184

Ryo straightened up and flexed his aching muscles. He was well aware that there was a strong circumstantial link between the murders of Nate Briggs and the gang of Goons because of the use of the unique particle beam weapons, but he still lacked a motive for the slaughter.

Commander Frédéric Rameau certainly seemed to be the key.

Ryo stood stiffly and finally decided to go home for the night. He would try to resolve the final inconsistencies over the next few days.

The Zmuda had been right about Rameau, Ryo realized as he turned off the lights, locked the door and shuffled down the dark hallway. The Lieutenant had assured him that the CRAMP was poised to somehow alleviate the Rameau problem.

• • •

"Welcome to the team," Jasper smiled to Lev as they bumped along together in the back seat.

"Thanks, I think." The lanky young man stared with growing misgivings out of the creaky open-air off-road carriage at the dry and forbidding vastness of the southern Sahara Desert.

From the driver's seat Mixion smirked at the novice spy.

185

"Ryo talked me into it," Lev mentioned to his new cohorts. "After he rescued my mother from the pirates, I'd do pretty much anything for him."

Mixion's head bobbed up and down in agreement. "It's really going to help us to put an end to the misdeeds of the EurAfrican racketeers and terrorists."

When Lev didn't seem to understand the unusually spiteful tone of the generally well-mannered woman, Jasper leaned over and whispered an explanation; "When she was only two, her mum was killed by thugs in Australia. It was really traumatic."

Lev nodded sympathetically, "I nearly lost *my* mom to the pirates."

Mixion silently studied the two men in the rear view mirror as she drove.

"Originally, Zmuda was supposed to be the third member on this little road trip out to the desert ruins." Jasper grinned at the woman and straightened up, "Since the Lieutenant was banged up a bit during the attack at the nightclub and we're still not entirely sure if the EurAfrican Military people really know who he is, Ryo recommended that you fill-in for the Lieutenant."

"Lucky me," Lev cringed.
186

• • •

The slave stared in surprise at the tattered note tucked between two folded pairs of trousers in his tiny room at the Domestic Servitude Housing Block.

He discreetly palmed the paper and casually checked the hallway and then the courtyard just beyond his window for others.

No one seemed to be lurking about in the Housing Block.

It had been agreed upon long ago that his CRAMP cohorts would only send him messages in the most dire of situations. Now he quivered with dread at actually receiving one. The contents could not be good.

The chance discovery of the note by the perpetually suspicious EurAfrican Military personnel who poked around relentlessly at the Base would certainly result in his swift execution.

For many minutes he busied himself brushing a thin accumulation of dust off of the wide windowsill. The man had never entirely satisfied himself that his room was free of surveillance devices. In the hyper-paranoid world of spies, one could never be too careful.

Torn From On High

He finally decided that he would curl up on his cot with the secret note and pretend to doze off.

With great effort he began to count his heartbeats as he lay nearly motionless. At an estimated 70 beats per minutes his goal was to wait until he'd tallied 1,400 beats, which would take around twenty minutes.

At 357 beats an old song from his past crept into his head. The task became much less monotonous with the ethereal musical accompaniment.

Oh, Rhonda you look so fine and I know it wouldn't take much time
For you to help me Rhonda, help me get her out of my heart...

He ran through the old surfer's tune many times.

When at last he'd reached 1,400 beats, he twisted around still feigning sleep and draped the hand that contained the now sweat-soaked message in front of his face.

He opened his eyes just enough to read the message.

Annoyingly, the note was upside-down but he was still able to make out the words.

It was handwritten in an unusual euphemistic
188

version of Street Spanish from the mid-Twenty-first century that he knew quite well from his childhood in Magdalena, New Mexico.

He carefully reread it many times, parsing each word and memorizing the exact phrasing for later analysis.

When he was satisfied that he would not forget any detail or nuance of the communiqué that had undoubtedly been delivered to him at great risk to the messenger, he slid his hand sleepily over his mouth and ingested the tattered paper.

He rolled over and considered the words, translated into English it worked out to this: *Your snarling dog bites too much! The cops want him put down!*

Before he'd left Free City, when he still had full use of his vocal cords, they'd discussed many scenarios and schemes in the CRAMP headquarters. This was one of the most daunting and dangerous directives that had been put forth. He knew that Zmuda would not have ordered it without compelling reasons.

He was to kill Commander Rameau at *any* cost.

• • •

"There it is, boys!" Mixion called out from the driver's seat.

Torn From On High

Just ahead on a flat stone outcropping in the blazing midday heat was the ancient mud brick ruins of the Fort of Djaba. The long-ago desiccated remains of what had likely been a lush oasis surrounded the derelict outpost.

"I don't see our Desert Serfs," Jasper noted.

Mixion parked the vehicle conspicuously in the middle of a wide, flat wash, "I'm sure they will find us soon enough."

Lev gathered the camera and clipboard.

"Remember," Mixion cautioned the men, "we're just 'grad students' doing some research." She sternly added, "We *must* all leave here alive within the next few hours."

Jasper nodded off-handedly but Lev cringed at the warning.

For twenty minutes the trio kept up their ruse as they photographed and surveyed the long forsaken site.

All three were certain that someone was watching them from the dense dry cover of the surrounding brush.

"Alright; let's get a few pictures of the north side of the watchtower," Mixion told the men.

The unmistakable metallic click of rifle bolts being engaged echoed around the ruins.

"YOU!"

Two gun-toting Desert Serfs emerged from the parched vegetation.

"No one is allowed here!"

Both Lev and Jasper bowed subserviently to the white-robed guards.

The diminutive Mixion stood her ground and stared with an ever-widening grin at the well-armed men, "Well; good morning!"

The surly sentinels faltered a bit at the sight of the gregarious young woman.

"What are you doing here?" demanded one of the Serfs.

"We're from the School of Anthropology at Free City University," Mixion produced a dog-eared certificate attesting to their identities. "We are doing a preliminary survey of historical sites in the northeastern District of Agadez. I have traveling papers signed by the District Minister himself."

She handed the documents to the man who was obviously in charge.

Torn From On High

"It's quite a lovely day," the woman noted as the Serfs studied the credentials.

Jasper nodded innocently along with the woman.

The subordinate guard whispered something about killing the intruders. His companion scowled and shook his head.

"Can we get a photo of you two in front of the Fort?" the woman coaxed. "I'd love show the District Minister that a couple of strapping locals are protecting the site."

Lev finally relaxed, Mixion's irresistible charm seemed to be slowly winning over the gun-toting Serfs.

"One picture only," the headman handed the paperwork back to her with a salacious grin. "I must insist that you leave straight away afterwards."

"Certainly," Mixion purred.

With near perfect showmanship, she directed the two men to pose with their ancient long rifles in front of the dilapidated Fort.

Jasper snapped a single photo as Lev diligently scribbled a few notes on the clipboard.

Mixion grinned at the sentinels, "Thank you so
192

much, gentlemen. We should be heading back this way in a day or so, perhaps we will stop by and visit again." She innocently offered her hand to the headman.

After several seconds of uncertainty, he finally clasped it with no small amount of lasciviousness.

"I look forward to your return."

Mixion, Lev and Jasper ambled back to their vehicle, all quite aware that a volley of gunfire might yet dispatch them.

"You drive;" Mixion whispered to Lev, "slow and friendly. We don't want to blow it in the last few minutes."

Lev climbed in to the driver's seat. Jasper stowed the camera and clipboard and he and Mixion slid into to the back seat with exaggerated caution.

Jasper waved amiably to the two Serfs as they puttered away.

The off-road vehicle stopped nearly a kilometer from the Fort.

Lev nervously glanced back and forth between the surrounding desert and his two companions in the backseat.

Mixion had been holding her right arm awkwardly upward, well away from anything else since just after they'd left the ruins.

Jasper retrieved a pair of green surgical gloves and a roll of clingy plastic wrap from under the seat.

"Hurry, Jasp!" the woman uncharacteristically barked.

The big Australian deftly encased her now trembling hand and arm in several protective layers of the flimsy material.

When the wrapping was secured in place with several strips of white adhesive tape she finally relaxed a bit.

"I really didn't think that we'd be able to pull off that charade," she sighed with visible relief.

Jasper kissed her on the cheek. "You were great, sweetheart."

"So were you two," a huge grin erupted on her face.

Jasper nodded, "Let's get the hell out of here."

• • •

Undoubtedly his cohorts back at the CRAMP headquarters had uncovered some compelling reason to justify the nearly impossible task. It certainly wasn't going to be easy; the slave ruminated as he scrubbed down the sweat-stained seat cushions in Commander Rameau's office.

Somehow he was going have to kill the EurAfrican Commander of Covert Operations, apparently the sooner the better. This was a military base filled with well-armed soldiers and suspicious intelligence officers and he was merely a General Facilities slave, which was about as harmless and expendable as they come.

Still, the man fretted, there had to be some way to dispatch the Commander without casting blame onto himself.

He was particularly interested in surviving the effort to murder Rameau.

Before he'd left Free City, Lieutenant Zmuda had assured him that several schemes were afoot to safely extract him from the Base in Tunis when his mission was completed.

He dearly hoped that he'd be extracted alive.

Earlier in the day, he'd considered poisoning Rameau's morning coffee but that seemed far too amateurish. In short order someone would likely trace the tainted beverage back to him. His execution would undoubtedly follow.

Similarly, strangling or stabbing the Commander, while effective, would inexorably result in his own death.

There *had* to be a better way.

The slave finished up his cleaning task and slid the chair into place neatly behind the desk. He stiffly straightened up and gathered his supplies.

And there it was on the desk.

He slowly dabbed his forehead and yawned to cover his growing fascination with the gray, steely object.

It was a weapon, he decided, the twenty-fifth century equivalent of a handgun.

The slave's fixation on the sidearm that was only one of many objects that cluttered Rameau's desk was cut short when he heard the short-tempered Commander clattering down the hallway.

He clutched his supplies and hastily left.

Somehow, he now knew, the weird weapon would figure in Rameau's impending death.

28. Checkmate

The Desert Serfs watched the old vehicle with the Free City Grad students rumble away.

Qadir turned to Tariq, "We should have killed them, my friend."

Tariq's dark eyes narrowed at the comment by his workmate, "They are harmless. One should not swat at every gnat that the wind happens to blow by."

Qadir persisted, "With luck, the foul-tempered Warlord whom we have hidden so well in the caves will merely lash us for insubordination and not behead us for this grave disobedience."

The vehicle receded from view.

Tariq slipped the ancient leather strap of the rifle over his shoulder, "You worry too much. We will not bother the Warlord with this minor anomaly."

Qadir stood taciturn for several seconds considering the words of his workmate; the man seemed to know the Warlord far better than anyone. Perhaps he was right.

He trotted after his companion as they resumed their sentry duty around the ruins.

Torn From On High

The two men walked for many minutes in silence through the dried oasis and out into the narrow stretch of open desert that led to the caves.

Finally Tariq spoke, "She is a beautiful woman."

Qadir nodded.

"This last year spent only with men has caused me to forget how enchanting the fair blossoms can be."

Tariq stopped suddenly and grinned, "If she returns, perhaps I will woo her."

Qadir laughed at his workmate, "A grimy EurAfrican Serf like you and a pretty little Free City maiden? I think that you would have better luck with the mangy old streetwalkers in Tunis."

"Ah;" Tariq smiled pleasantly, "it never hurts to try."

• • •

Far to the south, during a brief respite from the incessant icy wind that howls across South Georgia Island, Keira hugged Seamus just in front of the little white cottage perched above the harbor at New Grytviken.

He kissed her cheek with his cold, thin lips, "Thank you, my dear for delivering an old coot

198

to his new home."

Keira's eyes were misty, "Take care of yourself, Seamus."

As he watched from the porch, Luis smiled at the two while they said their goodbyes. They seemed almost like a revered grandfather and adored granddaughter, he realized.

She sniffled a bit and finally turned to trudge down the hill towards the landing pad.

Seamus's shoulders slumped as he stood stiffly against the wind and watched the woman board the patrol craft.

Luis was quite certain that the old man would live out his final days in New Grytviken.

With a steadily building roar, the patrol craft lifted off and dashed away.

Seamus waved halfheartedly to the receding ship and then hobbled back up the steps. He stared pleadingly at Luis, "For the second time in my life, I've lost everything. After I retired from work as the Chief Engineer on the *Billikin,* I had no one. I moved to Free City and eventually met a few nice folks." His shoulders slumped, "Now that's gone too."

Torn From On High

"Come on inside," Luis smiled to the downtrodden old man, "you'll always have me and Moresby on South Georgia Island."

• • •

There had been some mention of an unusual new gun by Zmuda just before he'd left Free City, the slave recalled. 'A strange new type of particle beam weapon,' the Lieutenant had said. The Spy Master had shown him some drawings and a few fuzzy snapshots of the mysterious gun.

The slave dug around in the janitor's closet for supplies.

Officially he was seeking some floor cleaner so that he'd be able to mop the long hallway, but in reality he hoped to find something that would aid in his efforts to kill the Commander.

He spotted a clear jug that contained a thin yellowish liquid. The slave glanced down the hallway before he opened the receptacle. The contents exuded a sharp, acidy stink. Petroleum distillates of some sort, he decided, perhaps naphtha or paraffin oil. Both had been used for centuries to remove tar and grease stains.

He capped the jug and set it aside.

Most of the rest of the cleaners and disinfectants in the closet were water-based and therefore useless for what he had in mind.

Near the back of the closet was a small and tattered box that was labeled with a fat red exclamation point to warn off the illiterate. It contained small soft white granules that resembled laundry detergent. He detected a distinct odor of ammonia and urea.

The slave spent several seconds examining the labeling on the box. Much of it was written in the odd and indecipherable new language called *rEn sprak* or *People Speak* that was spreading throughout AmerAsia.

He slowly smiled when he spotted the molecular formula near the bottom of the backside:

$CH_5N_3O_4/(NH_4)(NO_3)/Filler{:}CaCO_3/Trace{:}H_2O.$

This smelly, soapy powder and the yellowish liquid would make up the majority of what he would need.

• • •

Several hours later the slave had perfected the crude explosive in his tiny room in Housing Block 43.

As he had occasionally done in the past, he had taken several short walks out amongst the deserted landscape that made up this corner of the base. When he was certain that no one was around, he had set off tiny test explosions. Fortunately none were much louder than a single firecracker and of course they were barely noticeable compared to the incessant noise of the firing range a kilometer or so away.

Now he carefully cobbled together a small bomb.

The yellowish liquid caused the soapy powder to clump together into a grainy and oily blob. He estimated that he would need a quantity about the size of a small chicken egg.

Shortly he would add the final two key elements: A pea-sized piece of Y28 plastic explosive detonator that resembled a reddish-brown clump of chewing gum and a tiny glass bulb that contained two wires and a bead of mercury.

The bulb was called a Mercury Displacement Switch, although it reminded him of a single miniature Christmas tree light from his youth.

Both had been carefully hidden in his sandals many months ago by the CRAMP before he began his life as a slave in Mogadishu. He smiled a bit at the clever deception, stowing explosives in shoes had been commonplace during the twenty-first century but apparently no one had yet conceived of it in the mid twenty-fifth century.

The Mercury Displacement Switch was an absurdly simple device: Laid on its side, the silvery liquid metal was well away from the wire leads inside of the glass bulb. But if it was tipped upright, the Mercury connected the two wires together to complete the circuit. It would allow a spark to jump through the lump of detonator material and set off his homemade bomb.

The effort was not only likely to kill Rameau but also would destroy the unusual handgun.

He set aside his small cache of improvised explosives and retrieved the tiny radio transmitter hidden in the pair of pants that dangled from the clothesline.

The slave methodically tapped out a new message: ATMPTNG2KILDOG.

If the first effort to murder Rameau went either very well or terribly wrong, the slave ruminated, this could easily be his final message sent with the tiny transmitter.

He activated the device.

In about three hours he would endeavor to murder the Commander.

• • •

Torn From On High

"There he is!" Lev reported from the driver's seat of the rusty off-road vehicle.

Jasper and Mixion strained to spot the Lieutenant as they were jostled about in the backseat.

Zmuda sat in the dappled shade provided by a few old palms next to a similar old vehicle with the motor access hatch propped open.

Lev pulled next to the apparently malfunctioning machine.

The Lieutenant trotted up to greet them, "How did it go?"

Mixion smiled and held up her well-wrapped arm. "It took longer than we expected and for a few minutes I thought that we might be shot in the back but we made it."

"Good, good," Zmuda helped the woman from the backseat. "Let's see what you picked up."

For the next hour the Lieutenant repeatedly pealed back small sections of the wrap and painstakingly swabbed the freshly uncovered sections of the woman's hand and arm.

He would then pass the collected specimen to Jasper who would insert it into an Erie Instruments Chromosomal Comparator.

Lev stood guard on a low ridge about fifty meters away.

Six minutes after sliding the eleventh sample into the machine, a cheery 'ding' announced conclusive results.

Zmuda joined the big Australian and the two contemplated the message on the Comparator's display screen.

"Definitive Match. Margin of error > .001%," lazily flashed on the display.

"Just as we suspected;" Zmuda noted, "the Desert Serfs come into regular contact with Daniel Kufuzu, the recently recloned and still very well hidden Warlord of EurAfrica."

"Do you need anymore samples?" Mixion wondered.

"No; we've certainly found what we were looking for."

The woman nodded and removed the long plastic strip from her arm.

Jasper stowed the Comparator, whistled loudly to Lev and beckoned him to join them.

When the three junior spies had gathered around the Lieutenant, he produced an ordinary looking bottle of what appeared to be conventional sun block lotion.

"This is a particularly potent toxin custom tailored to kill *only* Daniel Kufuzu."

Lev stared at Zmuda in disbelief.

"The CRAMP has been working on variations of this for a few years now," the Lieutenant lectured the young man. "Mixion used an earlier form to kill off Dimitri Verhovnyi at the Warlord's palace on Titan about a year ago."

The woman recoiled at the mention of Verhovnyi; "I had to repeatedly stroke the bare flesh of that pig to get enough of the toxin onto him."

Lev tipped his head in dismay, "How are we going to do that with Daniel Kufuzu? The Desert Serfs are certainly not going to reveal where he is."

"No need;" snorted Jasper, "that earlier stuff was the x-pathogen." He tapped on the bottle, "This is a much more virulent version called the y-pathogen."

Zmuda nodded, "All that you have to is to put a small amount on your hands and especially your fingertips just before you meet up with the

Desert Serfs again. Try to touch them or any of their possessions as much as possible."

"Like ants returning to the colony with poisoned bait," Jasper continued, "the Serfs will bring the toxin to Kufuzu."

"In short order he will die of what appears to be a lethal bout of pneumonia."

Lev stroked his chin in thought for several seconds, "What if they just reclone him again?"

"It won't help," Mixion grinned. "Since the Serfs will become unwitting carriers for life, they will spread the Kufuzu-specific y-pathogen wherever they go. It will lay dormant for centuries. If another clone is produced, he too will die within days."

"Mmm;" Lev stared at the bottle, "hopefully no one ever cooks up a Lev Fesai variation."

• • •

In the middle of his desk, an oil-stained note was laid haphazardly on top of the small particle beam weapon.

Rameau glared at the message, 'Fred, Why was this side arm left on your desk? Lock it up at once! Major Gen SJLeBoc.'

"Friggin' bastard!" Fredric growled. He did not

appreciate his direct superior meddling in his matters.

Rameau set the note aside.

A sharp, acidy urine-like smell caught his attention.

Yellow liquid had formed a tiny pool just below the handle of the irreplaceable weapon.

Perhaps, Rameau reasoned, Bowie or one of the other Goons had damaged one of the internal components.

He gingerly gripped the barrel and lifted the gun.

Rameau tipped the weapon to peek at the underside.

Just inside the handgrip the inexorable chain of events took only a fraction of a second to run its course.

The change in orientation caused the miniscule bead of mercury to flow over the two bare wires completing the circuit. A 90-volt spark arced through a pea-sized lump of Y28 plastic explosive detonator producing a small pop and a great deal of heat. The flammable mixture containing naphtha molded around the detonator instantly ignited. Fanned by the oxygen-rich powdered nitrates, the oily glob exploded.

208

The small explosion shattered the antimatter power cell that had supplied the initial charge in the handle of the weapon.

The infinitesimal clump of several dozen iron antimatter atoms safely suspended by magnets in the center of the vacuum-tight power cell was abruptly hurled against the conventional matter casing.

Antimatter unforgivingly annihilates matter and the result was a nuclear explosion in miniature.

Before he was even aware of the horrid chain of events, Commandeer Frédéric Rameau received a fatal dose of ultra high-energy gamma rays.

Two microseconds later the blast tore him apart.

29. Escape!

Even though he'd been expecting the explosion, the slave flinched when it finally happened.

The sturdy office building creaked and swayed for several seconds.

Smoke and dust was everywhere.

He'd been waiting patiently for hours in the Janitor's closet at the far end of the hallway. Seven minutes ago the Commander had returned to his office.

Now the slave had to suppress the urge to rush towards the office to assure himself of the man's death. He took a deep breath and began to slowly count down from thirty. Being overly eager to check on the results of the explosion would likely sprinkle him with a lethal dose of lingering radiation.

Alarms sounded.

A horrified corporal dashed into the mangled office.

The young soldier screeched in agony.

Was it the carnage or searing residual radiation that had caused the outburst?

210

The corporal reappeared with horrible bloody lesions on his ruddy red face.

"HE'S DEAD!" the man shrieked.

The slave nodded slightly from the comparative safety of the Janitor's closet door, he had his answer.

Now he must escape.

• • •

Clutching a ragged floor mop, mainly as prop to highlight his apparent innocence, the slave staggered out of Building 17 at the EurAfrican Imperial Military Base.

Firefighters and well-armed Base sentries pushed their way past him.

He stumbled around theatrically for several seconds, even pointing dumbly at the building before dropping his mop and teetering off toward the Housing Block. Beyond that goal, he had no idea of where he would go.

Several hundred meters away, between Buildings 3 and 4, a white-clad bakery Serf caught his arm.

The slave stared in wide-eyed fear at the stout man.

"Come with me," the baker whispered, "Zmuda will want to hear of this."

Hours later the mute former slave was standing circumspectly at the bow of the midmorning ferry boat dressed as a nondescript businessman making the crossing from Tunis to Sicily. His savior, the baker, was similarly attired and kept a close eye on the smattering of other travelers.

The spy turned slave turned spy again watched the watery tumult caused by the bow as it sliced through the bluish-gray water of the Mediterranean Sea. Angry white waves roiled away from the ship and slowly flattened out into long receding ribbons of pearly foam.

He finally grinned at his startling success; hopefully his CRAMP cohorts were enjoying similarly good luck.

30. News Item: Incident at Military Base

Dateline: 29th of September, 2446; Tunis, EurAfrica, Earth.

Stubborn rumors persist regarding some sort of accident inside the sprawling EurAfrican Imperial Military Base in Tunis late yesterday. Accounts vary widely amongst sources both semi-official and otherwise but all indicate that at least one high-ranking officer and perhaps several enlisted personnel perished after a blast destroyed an office.

Public Relations Officer Captain Rumford Johnson acknowledged only that a handgun apparently misfired and caused some unexpected damage. The official press release this morning indicated that an "unexpained anomaly" had occurred in Building 17.

Several unnamed Serfs working in adjoining buildings revealed that significant radiation was released requiring many bystanders to endure decontamination following the incident.

Sirens could be erratically heard for hours at the base following the explosion. Local residents just outside the main gates were briefly warned to stay inside. The order was lifted thirty minutes later without explanation.

Base investigators continue to search through the wreckage.

31. The games people play

It had taken them nearly two days to return to the ruins of the Fort of Djaba, Jasper noted as he wearily studied the long-forsaken site.

Lev and Mixion were using an antique transit and elevation rod to map the site. Jasper was halfheartedly scribing their measurements into an old logbook.

Days earlier Lieutenant Zmuda had hastily left them at the desert rendezvous site just after they had discovered that Mixion had picked up traces of Daniel Kufuzu's DNA from the Desert Serfs guarding the ruins.

A late afternoon sand storm had precluded their own departure and the threesome decided to put off the return to the Fort until conditions improved.

He, Mixion and Lev Fesai were now exhausted.

Last night they had endured a nearly unbearable 'camp out' in the open desert. The trio had scarcely prepared for that scenario beforehand and had not packed suitable provisions for the day and a half that they hunkered together in a tiny backpacker's tent.

The three junior spies were now low on water

and their creaky old vehicle currently contained a disturbing amount of wind-blown sand.

All were hungry, dirty and disheveled.

They had received a cryptic message from Zmuda earlier in the morning indicating that he was back at Free City University teaching his classes and studying the small particle beam weapon that he had purloined from the nightclub in New Rome.

The bone-weary spies had arrived at the ruins three hours ago and each had applied a generous amount of the fake sun block lotion containing the y-pathogen to their hands and arms. They hoped it would dispatch the clone of Daniel Kufuzu that the Desert Serfs had hidden somewhere nearby.

Mixion had decided that they would stay at the site for days if necessary until the Serfs returned. The effort to kill Kufuzu was so important that they could not depart until the guards had been contaminated with the toxin.

She morbidly pointed out that even if the men killed them, the Serfs would likely become infected after meddling with their corpses.

Lev had been visibly shocked by that assertion.

• • •

A rustling of dry foliage caused Mixion to swivel around from the surveyor's transit.

"And so you are back," the Desert Serf bowed as he emerged from cover of the surrounding brush.

This time, she noted, the head Serf was alone and his long rifle was strapped harmlessly across his back.

She smiled at him and returned his bow. "Yes; we were waylaid many kilometers to the northwest by a rather drawn out sandstorm."

He studied her for several seconds; "You look rather the worst for it, my little dove."

"I'm afraid so," she sighed.

Jasper ambled to her side.

Mixion noticed that the Serf seemed annoyed at the intrusion of the big Australian. Perhaps she could use his obvious interest in her to their advantage.

"Jasper," she started, "what do we have in the old clunker that we could possibly trade for some water?" She stared with great intensity at him until he finally realized that she was attempting to manipulate the situation.

"Oh; let me see," he thought for a moment,

"we've got a spare flashlight, a two week old edition of the Nairobi Times and three stale chocolate bars."

She turned back to the Desert Serf, "What would it take to get a canteen filled with good drinking water, my friend?"

"Please call me Tariq," he grinned at the effort to bargain with him. "I believe that I will require all of these things that you speak of for merely half a canteen drawn from the more brackish of our two wells."

Mixion nodded in earnest, "I suppose we will replenish our water in Séguedine." She pivoted toward the vehicle.

"Wait;" Tariq caught her arm.

Mixion smiled at her luck; the man had unwittingly picked up at least a modest amount of the y-pathogen from the lotion on her skin. She turned to face him again.

He stared at her with deep simmering brown eyes.

"Perhaps I have asked too much to help a lovely young maiden such as you." The man struggled to contain his desire for the woman. "If you will stay for a time, I will exchange some good water for your chocolate."

218

Mixion studied him beguilingly. "I believe we have a deal," she offered her hand to seal the agreement.

Tariq eagerly clasped the woman's hand and she readily squeezed it to transfer still more of the pathogen onto him.

"If you will give me your canteen, I shall fill it for you. When I return we will have a feast of chocolate and a dozen or so figs that I have collected in the last few months."

"Certainly," she replied cheerily.

• • •

Seamus was obviously enjoying himself.

They'd been playing halfpenny ante poker for hours with a sack of the antique English coins that Luis had unearthed years earlier while repairing some storm damage in the New Grytviken cemetery.

The two men had become fast friends since Keira had delivered Seamus to the far-flung island. They spent most of their waking hours chatting about their lives or tending to minor duties at the facility. Seamus had even grown fond of Moresby, Luis's stalwart old cat.

Luis grinned at his lucky hand of cards and slid a

fat copper coin across the table, "I'll see your bet and raise you a half, old man."

"Hah, mighty brave for a lad who's been on a long losing streak," Seamus teased. He added a half pence of his own to the mound. "What do you have, sonny boy?"

Luis could barely contain himself, "Sevens and twos in a lovely full house."

"Yikes; you've got me!" Seamus spread his cards on the table, "Three Jacks."

Luis raked his winning into a small pile.

The old man took a sip of the lemonade that they had reconstituted just for the occasion from the decades-old provisions left behind by the previous caretaker.

"If the sea ice isn't too bad, I'm going to take the grappler tug out on the bay tomorrow and clear out some driftwood. Did you want to come along?"

Seamus dabbed his chin with a tattered old hand towel before answering, "The weather's supposed to be windy and below freezing in the morning, I think my old joints will be too stiff to venture outside. Perhaps the cat and I will sleep off this debauchery."

Luis retrieved the cards and began to shuffle, "Suit yourself."

• • •

True to his word, Tariq returned an hour later dangling the canteen by the strap.

Mixion had instructed Jasper to feign taking a nap in the off-road vehicle. She would shout if the Desert Serf presented any problems. Lev sat in the shade of a palm fifteen meters away slowly reading through the old edition of the Nairobi Times. He too was at the ready should difficulties arise.

Tariq held the canteen temptingly in front of her. He likely had handled it sufficiently to pick up plenty of the toxin that covered the surface. If he'd filled it by immersing the container in the well, as was the custom in the desert, the water source would spread the pathogen to anyone who used it for centuries to come. Hundreds of future users of the water source would be unknowing agents in the effort to kill clones of Daniel Kufuzu.

She smiled at the apparent success that the unwitting man had likely provided for them.

The woman gave him the three heat-softened chocolate bars, "Here you go. I believe we have both received a tremendous bargain."

Torn From On High

Tariq nodded and produced a handful of figs.

The petite spy and the rugged desert dweller enjoyed each other's company for about two hours as they shared the food and water near the tumbled-down Fort of Djaba.

At 3 PM they parted ways, both quite certain that they'd gotten the better of the other.

• • •

On the day after Tariq had his brief and seemingly innocent liaison with the beguiling black woman from Free City, Daniel Kufuzu fell ill.

At first the Warlord complained of a sore throat. By noon the man was racked with a hoarse cough and delirious with a high fever.

Tariq and his workmates struggled to make the man comfortable.

At sunset Kufuzu lapsed into a coma.

Qadir trotted off towards Séguedine in search of a doctor.

Sometime around midnight Daniel Kufuzu, the recently recloned and highly Exalted Warlord of EurAfrica succumbed to the custom-made version of the y-pathogen that Tariq had

222

unwittingly carried into the secret cave in the
Saharan Desert.

At midday, they wrapped his body in a white
shroud and buried him in a hastily dug pit in the
desert.

32. Fret

Luis stared doggedly ahead through the blowing snow as the grappler tug plodded between the chunks of sea ice that blocked much of Cumberland East Bay. A half-kilometer ahead were the docks of New Grytviken and beyond that up on the bluff was his little white cottage.

He had managed to clear much of the driftwood that had been pushed into the harbor by the relentless wind and the advancing sea ice. Several immense logs were bobbing along behind the tug, lashed together with steel cable chokers and a few stout chains. Most of the smaller debris was piled amid ship on the deck. In a day or two when the weather let up, he'd drag the driftwood onshore with a winch and add it to the huge heap that was slowly rotting just south of the docks.

Seamus had been right, Luis realized, the weather was far too cold and stormy to be out on the bay in a small craft.

He eased the tug towards the dock. A good five meters of floating ice stood between the little ship and the ancient wooden piles of the dock. This would be a problem; if he couldn't secure the tug firmly to the stout dock bollards then the small craft would be battered against the ice by

the waves and wind. The hull would surely be
pierced and the invaluable tug would be lost.

Luis put the motor into neutral and stepped out
onto the deck to examine the problem.

He stared at the thick, puzzle-pieced blocks of
ice for many minutes.

Perhaps he could use the long articulating arm of
the deck-mounted knuckle crane to force the ice
sideways and away from the dock. It would be
difficult and time-consuming but he realized
there was no other way that he could accomplish
his task.

Luis activated the auxiliary steering controls at
the console next to the crane and set to work
nudging the huge chunks of ice away from the
dock.

• • •

"What is it?" Jana tilted her head in concern.

Her date with Ryo wasn't going well.

He fidgeted sullenly as they sat together awaiting
their food at the posh *La Planche à Laver* bistro.

She'd had a rare break in her normally swamped
schedule at the University and decided to spend
some time with him.

225

Now she was rather regretting the decision.

"I'm sorry," he smiled halfheartedly. "Some of the particulars of this investigation have caused me to question whether I should have returned to police work."

Jana frowned, "Is it serious?"

Ryo restlessly straightened the knife and spoon on the napkin before answering, "That's the problem, I'm just not sure."

He stared moodily at her for several seconds. "On the night of the grenade blast in New Rome, when I first came upon the thugs who eventually caused all of the death and destruction, one of the fellows rattled off a long string of personal details about me."

"What sort of details?"

"Most of it was standard stuff, age and rank, that type of thing. But he also knew my home address and apartment number. The Inquisitor's Office goes to great lengths to protect that information."

"Well; he *is* dead now," Jana tried to assure him, "so it shouldn't be a problem."

Ryo shook his head, "He was part of a gang and there is still one punk left."

She slipped her hand over his putting an end to his fidgeting, "I've seen you in action, you're a pretty tough guy."

"You're right, I suppose. But that's not the problem." His shoulders slumped, "I'm worried about Dilma."

• • •

After hours of exhausting effort Luis had finally managed to tie up the grappler tug. The huge driftwood logs that trailed out behind the vessel clattered unsettlingly against the dock pilings.

It was numbingly cold as he struggled stiffly up the creaky, frost-covered dock ladder.

He stopped halfway up as the wind and a wave surge caused the battered rocket booster to groan restlessly against its moorings fifteen meters further down the dock.

The overhead lights flickered briefly high up on the standards.

It all seemed to be a sinister omen.

Luis shivered as he clung to the ladder.

The wind subsided and the rocket booster settled back into the water with a protracted rasp of metal against wood.

227

Torn From On High

He resumed his ascent.

When Luis finally made it to the dock a harsh
gust of freezing wind threw him off balance and
he tumbled awkwardly.

A hollow snapping sound in his left ankle
preceded the intense pain that shot up his leg.

Luis writhed on the slick wooden planks. The
throbbing was excruciating. His toes were
already numb; constricted by his tight-fitting
boot, the rapid swelling had cut off the blood
supply.

He sprawled in agony on the frozen dock for
many minutes. Somehow he had to get back to
the cottage. Surely Seamus would nurse him
back to health.

Finally Luis crawled to the nearest of the derelict
buildings clustered around the boat dock.

Ironically, he realized as he dragged himself
through the door, this was where he'd kept Nate
Briggs' corpse after he'd freed the man's remains
from the rocket booster.

It was nearly six hours later when Luis hobbled
up the front porch stairs of the darkened cottage
using a pair of crutches that he'd improvised
from some scrap water pipes wrapped with
several rags for padding.

He pushed open the door and called for his
housemate.

Not surprisingly, he heard no answer. Seamus
was a particularly deep sleeper.

Luis struggled about until he found the old man.

Seamus was slumped unnaturally over one side
of the table that they'd used the night before for
the poker game.

His eyes were open and glassy. The old man's
skin was bluish-gray and already cold to the
touch.

Somehow, Seamus had died.

As his eyes teared-up at the terrible loss, Luis
realized that he was once again alone on South
Georgia Island.

• • •

In the dingy Records Room at the Inquisitor's
Office, Ryo groaned a bit as he decided that this
latest stack of documents had led him to another
dead end.

In the many days since he had discovered that
Commander Frédéric Rameau had been
responsible for directing the Goons in their

criminal activities, the old Investigator had still
not uncovered a firm motive for the crime wave.

The use of the unique particle beam weapons by
the Goons and the equally unique wounds on the
corpses of their many victims certainly tied the
gang to the mass murders. But what had been the
rationale for the slaughter?

It all seemed to circle back to Commander
Frédéric Rameau and, by extension, the
unendingly troublesome EurAfrican Imperial
Military.

Ryo was certain that Nate Briggs and the crew of
the *Billikin* had been murdered for reason, but as
of yet, that reason had eluded him.

Perhaps Lieutenant Zmuda could deduce why the
dead Commander would have wanted to kill off
an obscure Space Debris Retrieval Specialist in
Low Earth Orbit.

Ryo produced his communications device and
connected to his boss's office ten floors above
him.

"What is it, Inspector Trop?" Helga glanced
tersely at the screen as she read through some
documents.

"I'd like to head over to the CRAMP
headquarters and meet with Zmuda," he started.
230

"Don't bother;" she scowled, "he's in the Forensic Signal Processing Lab right now."

The screen abruptly went blank.

Ryo smiled a bit; finally some good luck.

Ten minutes later he pushed open the Lab door. The facility was utilitarian in the extreme, with dozens of mismatched racks of both antiquated and state-of-the-art gadgetry most of which were interconnected with chaotic tangles of black and gray cables.

He stepped over a small open crate that blocked the only obvious pathway through the maze of equipment.

Ryo ventured cautiously past a cluttered workbench with several odd and unidentifiable devices sporting blinking blue and yellow lights. Two of the machines seemed to flash back and forth to each other while they were apparently solving some sort of enigmatic matter.

Near the back of the overstuffed workroom, Ryo found the Lieutenant with Forensic Technician Second Class Nicola Jenks.

Zmuda beamed at Ryo's arrival, "Inspector, you're definitely going to like what Ms. Jenks has unearthed."

She smiled pleasantly at Ryo and tapped at a large wall-mounted display screen, "We extracted the radar information from the Salvage Ship *Billikin.*"

A fuzzy black and white image of wavy lines and indistinct shapes appeared.

Nicola pointed to a ghostly outline of a small runabout class spacecraft, "This is Mr. Nate Briggs in the *Dreg's Scamp* on the day of his death." Her finger slid down the screen to a large cylinder, "Based on the radio chatter at the time, I'm nearly certain that this is the rocket booster that was recovered in New Grytviken along with the decedent's body."

"Play the video for Inspector Trop," Zmuda prompted.

She set the image into motion.

A large net of some sort wafted away from the runabout and drifted towards the booster. An ethereal likeness of a man could be seen on the deck of the small craft.

"Now watch in the left hand corner," she said.

A small and nearly invisible vessel glided to within a hundred meters of Nate Briggs and stopped.

"What...?" Ryo wondered.

"Wait;" Zmuda held up his hand to stop him, "keep watching."

A very thin gray beam flashed from the stealthy vehicle and struck Nate Briggs just below his helmet. The net caught the booster. The apparently now debilitated junkman drifted limply away from the deck, attached only by a long lifeline. The ensnared rocket lurched downward pulling the runabout and Nate Briggs off the bottom of the screen.

The phantom craft that had set the whole catastrophe into motion sped away.

Nicola froze the picture with the mysterious vessel in the upper right corner.

"This footage has been *greatly* enhanced," she pointed to the still image, "in the unprocessed file the intruder is not visible at all. Certainly Captain Takahashi wouldn't have spotted it from the *Billikin*."

"I had a hunch about this when I first saw it," the Lieutenant said as he stared at the craft. "I came across a tidbit sometime ago from an operative at the Imperial Spaceport in Madagascar noting that the EurAfrican Military had launched a tiny stealth interceptor barely larger than a man."

He produced a blurry photograph and held it up to the screen, "We believe that *this* is that vessel."

Nicola nodded in agreement.

Ryo spent several minutes comparing the photo and the image on the screen. "So someone apparently snuck up on poor Mr. Briggs while he was tending to his job and shot at him with some sort of weapon. In short order he was pulled to his fiery demise. Weeks later, Harbor Master Luis Hernandez towed the badly singed rocket booster to the docks at New Grytviken and discovered Nate's remains."

"So it seems."

"I believe I know the answer already," the old Inspector turned to the others, "can you tell from the radar images what type of weapon was used in this attack?"

"Ah;" Nicola ran the video backwards to the point where the beam emanated from the tiny intruder, "this weapon's spectral discharge is unique. I was unable to discover any similar radiation patterns until the Lieutenant arrived about an hour and a half ago with some new data."

Zmuda grinned and produced the small particle beam weapon that he had recovered earlier in

New Rome. "Either this particular weapon or one of the two identical others was used in the attack on Nate Briggs."

Ryo studied the odd side arm, "How did you conclude that?"

The Lieutenant set the strange gun on to a cluttered workbench, "I have been testing this gruesome device for days. I did a routine spectrum analysis on Tuesday. Yesterday the spy that killed Commander Rameau in Tunis joined me in the Lab and he added several invaluable insights as to the internal workings of the weapon. Additionally the fellow indicated that he had personally seen records about the gunsmith who had produced the three copies of the unique weapon. Apparently Rameau had him killed to insure that there would be no further production of the guns."

"A small and very deadly weapon that no one else has," Ryo stroked his chin in thought.

Zmuda nodded, "It emits a very narrow stream of ultra high-speed neutrons. The amount of highly focused energy is quite extraordinary. In the thick atmosphere of Earth, say in a bar in New Rome, the effective range is maybe 5 meters. In space, without the encumbrance of atmospheric gases, the range is almost infinite."

Ryo frowned as he considered the complicated

train of logic presented by the evidence. "There is an unlikely chance that one or more of the weapons was stolen but everything else points to Commander Frédéric Rameau procuring the three unique weapons and engaging the services of the Goons to kill Nate Briggs and, very likely, the crew members of the *Billikin*. Additionally, Mr. Schleim broke into Seamus Nelson's apartment and assaulted him with the intent of intimidation. Schleim was accidentally killed during the incident. Fellow gang members Fritzi Wolfe and Norman Rollo unintentionally murdered Liaison Agent Hugo Mackillroy during an ill-fated meeting at a nightclub in New Rome."

Nicola was aghast at Ryo's recounting of the brutality.

"The body count has been horrendous during this crime wave," Zmuda winced as he recalled the gruesome deaths at *The Hissing Serpent*.

"It's not over yet," Ryo ruminated, "there's one gun and one Goon left."

33. News Item: Unsettling times are afoot

Dateline: 3rd of October, 2446; Nairobi, EurAfrica, Earth

Times are changing and that is not a good thing for those of us with a fondness for the ways of the past.

Even the most apathetic citizens of EurAfrica are no doubt aware of the swift and lamentable developments that have befallen our once great Fiefdom. As a testament to this regrettable deterioration, this reporter has amassed three recent items from several different sources.

First; a young female exchange student from Free City was recently arrested in the Piazza District of New Rome on the misdemeanor charge of misappropriation of property. Neighbors reported that the woman had been hiding an especially tattered looking man in her room at a low-end boardinghouse. The rather naive woman claimed that the fellow was her lover. When Police intervened at the request of the landlord, they discovered that the bum was an escaped slave from Sienna.

As has been the custom of EurAfrican law enforcement for centuries, the arresting officers summarily executed the escaped slave in the street as a reminder to other drudges of the consequences of disobedience. The arresting officers were then set upon by thugs and rabble-rousers. A three daylong riot ensued in the District with dozens injured and five killed. Scores of local establishments were vandalized by roving mobs of malcontents, many of whom claimed that the slave *should* have been set free. An uneasy peace was restored only after a battalion of heavily armed soldiers was brought in from Tunis.

Secondly; much further to the south, Serfs affiliated with the Construction Trade Guild in the town of Windhoek in Southwest Africa engaged in the unheard-of and reprehensible act of striking for better working conditions and payment of past-due wages.

Windhoek is currently experiencing an unprecedented influx of new residents, many of whom were displaced last year with the destruction of Arusha. The demand for suitable housing has soared and the Association of Landlords has commissioned dozens of new apartment buildings. All of this has led to months of ceaseless work for the lowly Serfs of the Construction Trade Guild. Because of cash flow issues centering on a banking scandal in Southwest Africa, the funding for the new apartments has been anemic. The Association of

Landlords has threatened to bring in replacement workers to break the strike but most doubt it could be done successfully.

Finally in Nairobi; persons unknown have repeated vandalized the statues in the Panoply of Modern Heroes. The secretive mutilators have spared no statue bearing the name of Kufuzu. The representations of all four of the Warlords that have reigned over our beloved Fiefdom have been smashed, defaced or molested. Some inconclusive evidence for the crimes points to local Serfs and Enlightenment Crusade agitators from Free City.

The Curator of the Garden grumbled loudly that the Panoply of Modern Heroes might have to be closed unless the vandalism ceases. The treasures it contains would then be out of reach of all.

In all three of these cases, troublemakers from outside of our once great land have been largely to blame for the decline of the Supreme Imperial Fiefdom of EurAfrica.

34. Herman "Bowie" Kowalski

"Tell me about it again, Shayna."

The temporarily unemployed waitress from the
Hissing Serpent flirtatiously kissed his cheek,
"OK Bowie, one more time but then you gotta
hand over the twenty-five Units that you
promised me." She stroked his well-muscled
arm, "A girl's got to pay her rent, you know."

The only surviving member of the Goons
nodded, "Sure baby."

"Well there was these two guys from Free City,"
she started, "they were sitting in one of the back
booths when I was working the evening shift."

Bowie downed the whiskey on the rocks as he
listened.

"Your two pals; what were their names?"

The big man sneered a bit at the half-witted
waitress, "I told you ten times already, Wolfe
and Rollo!"

"Yeah; that's right Wolfe and Rollo, they were
sitting on either side of this third guy that they
kept calling Macaroni, but I don't think that was

really his name."

"Damn it!" Bowie slammed the empty glass onto the table, "Come on Shayna; get to the part just before the explosion!"

"OK, OK. There was a bet about who could drink what without puking. The old man sitting with them went to the bar and ordered a Dragon's Breath Rum. It's real nasty stuff. When he got back to the table there was some kind of argument and Wolfe pulled out this strange gun that he had. Then the old man flung the rum into Wolfe's eyes and cracked his gun hand on the table. The Free City jerks ran off like cowards with some young guy who was drinking at the bar. The next thing I know there was an explosion and I was out of a job."

"Did the gun look like this?" Bowie drew the last of the three weapons from his black jacket.

The dull-witted woman examined the side arm, "Yeah; just like that."

He slipped it back into his jacket. Bowie had to be particularly careful with the gun; the power indicator said that it had only enough energy for three more shots. With luck, that would be just right.

Bowie retrieved a payment interface and transferred the money to Shayna's account, "Not a word about this to anyone."

She nodded.

He produced a picture, "Was this the guy who roughed up Wolfe?"

"Sure; that's him," she finally answered after studying the image for several seconds. "What you gonna do about it, Bowie?"

The big man slipped the photo back into his jacket, "I'm going to make that bastard Ryo Trop pay for killing Wolfe and Rollo."

• • •

"Ah; this is it!" Ryo grinned.

He'd struggled mightily for weeks to discover a motive for the murder of Nate Briggs.

When criminal inquiries stalled Investigators were forced to go over mountains of minutia for new clues and that's exactly what he'd been doing.

Zmuda had sent over dozens of new documents from the CRAMP Headquarters that detailed the highly convoluted financial deals of the Kufuzu family since the death of Warlord Daniel Kufuzu.

Amongst other accounting shenanigans, he had traced several large payments to members of the Goons Gang back through a complex smoke screen of money laundering and double-dealing to EurAfrican Consolidated Metals and Mining.

The Warlord Syndicate had recently asked the Free City Inquisitor's Office to investigate allegations that Consolidated Metals was manipulating the prices of titanium and aluminum.

Both metals had recently experienced exorbitant run-ups in prices, all of which highly benefited EurAfrican Consolidated Metals and the Kufuzu family as its chief stakeholders.

The Goons had been paid off from a secret slush fund brazenly called "Salvage Intimidation."

Ryo tapped out an information request on his interface screen: *Quantity details of metals salvaged from Low Earth Orbit in the last six months.*

Several graphs appeared showing a steep decline in output beginning about four months ago. It was just about the same time that Nate had been killed, Ryo noted.

Along with the use and possession of the unusual weapons, the financial information meant that he had sufficient circumstantial evidence now to charge Bowie with Nate Briggs' murder.

Ryo summoned the All-Points Bulletin for Herman "Bowie" Kowalski to the screen and added several details: *Detain at all costs! Considered armed and extremely dangerous. If apprehended, contact Inspector First Class Ryo Trop IMMEDIATELY under the authority of Edict 343 and authorization of the Free City High Court.*

He posted the amended bulletin.

Hopefully Bowie would be found before anyone else died.

• • •

The big cargo transport was parked just down the Dublin street awaiting the return of the driver.

Bowie stood over the body of the dead deliveryman in the dark alley next to the man's most recent stop. His dagger was embedded to the hilt in the poor slobs chest. A river of ruby red blood gushed from the wound and pooled up on the pavement around the corpse.

He'd finally found the perfect victim. The deliveryman looked fairly similar to him, and more importantly, his route took him into Free City.

Bowie wrestled the dagger free and used it to methodically saw off the dead man's left index finger. He wrapped the bloody end with a rag and then carefully bound the spare digit between his own index and middle fingers.

With luck, this trick would get him past the border guards and into Free City.

Hours later in Free City, Bowie scowled as he stood in front of the beat up door of apartment 392. This was where the bastard lived.

He glanced up and down the long, dim hallway. No one was around; it was perfect for some strong-arm intimidation.

Bowie retrieved the bloodstained dagger that he'd used earlier in the day and, in one swift move, pounded it into the flimsy surface of the old door.

The tip of the dagger had splintered the thin veneer and penetrated most of the way through the door.

He smiled as he studied his work; it would surely scare the crap out of the old Investigator.

Bowie turned and sauntered off leaving his knife behind.

In a few days he'd start killing off the members of Ryo Trop's cozy little household.

Torn From On High

• • •

The girl frowned.

"Goodnight Daddy; I miss you," Dilma stared at him in consternation from the screen of his communication device, "come home soon."

"OK sweetie. Be good for Sabra and I'll see you in the morning."

The connection terminated and Ryo was left alone in the gloomy workroom at the Inquisitor's Office.

It had been an unsettling several days for his little family and this late night work session wasn't making things any easier.

Time was running out and he *had* to locate Herman 'Bowie' Kowalski and put an end to the disturbing case.

Three days ago his landlord had called him in a panic at work. Someone had driven a bloodstained dagger into the door of his apartment. Undoubtedly, Ryo had surmised, Bowie had been responsible for the act of vandalism.

Fortunately no one was at home during the misdeed.

Ryo then promptly sent several plain clothes Investigators out to the Connaught School to keep an eye out for trouble. He'd personally sprinted over to the University and located Sabra in the Ceramics Workshop.

The nanny was perplexed by his unexpected appearance.

In hushed tones he explained to her that, due to some difficulties of a current investigation, she and Dilma were to immediately take several days off and move into a safe house in the Eire District.

When Sabra bemoaned that she would miss an important examination in her *Alternative Lifestyles* class, Ryo tersely cut her off.

After several seconds of silent pouting, she seemed to finally understand the severity of the situation.

Now in the dark office, Ryo rubbed his forehead in dread as he shuffled through the paperwork on the desk. Bowie was trying to get to him and he had managed to find the only personal soft spot that the old Investigator had allowed himself in over thirty-five years: His feelings for Dilma.

• • •

Torn From On High

The mysterious redheaded woman stared at the message that slowly flashed on her communications device; it was a new assignment from Lieutenant Zmuda.

She studied the particulars, it would require about a day of careful preparation to pull off with the personal flair that she felt was fitting for her participation.

The woman made some quick decisions about what would be required and concluded that she would accept the assignment.

She pressed the *Acknowledge* button and set about making arrangements.

• • •

It was just past one in the morning when the door to Ryo's workroom at the Inquisitor's Office creaked open.

The old Investigator set aside the routine banking records.

A rather mousy-looking young woman peeked in, "Excuse me Mr. Trop, I was looking for the Chief Inspector but she's nowhere to be found."

It was Cadet Helen MacDermish.

Ryo waved her in. "Ah; let me check the roster."
248

He tapped on his interface screen. "She seems to have gone home for the evening, which I guess puts an end to the recent rumor that the Chief Inspector never sleeps."

Helen smiled at his quip.

"Maybe I can help you," Ryo volunteered.

"Well I don't know if it is important or not," she hedged, "but I've been checking over the routine paperwork regarding border crossings."

"Go on."

She nervously twisted the collection of papers that she was holding, "I had gone over the two hundred and twelve crossings from earlier in the week and cross-referenced them with both the Inquisitor's Office and EurAfrican All-Points databases and everything seemed to be normal."

The rookie produced a single sheet from her hoard.

Ryo studied the document. It was the standard printout detailing that a EurAfrican delivery driver named Manfred Chong crossed into the Free City Autonomous Zone at the rarely used Ballyshannon East Gate at 10:32AM yesterday morning. His cargo was mostly machine parts from Dublin.

Ryo set the paper aside, "What seems to be the problem, Ms MacDermish?"

"At first I thought it was a mistake, perhaps just a mix up with the names, but the more that I checked, the scarier it got." She handed him a second sheet.

It was a rather bloody crime scene photo. The date stamp indicated that a beat cop in Dublin had taken it at 4:13AM on the previous day.

Ryo stared at the young woman for several seconds, "I don't understand."

She quivered with pent-up agitation, "*That* is Manfred Chong, the delivery man. He'd been dead for over six hours when he supposedly crossed the border."

Ryo glanced at the macabre image, "Excellent work Helen. I will surely note your superb efforts to the Chief Inspector."

She had an odd look of confusion, "I'm sorry Mr. Trop, but I don't understand what's happened."

"Call me Ryo," he chuckled gleefully. "Let's dig into this anomaly together. Perhaps you have uncovered a significant lead."

She pulled up a chair and sat next to him at the ancient oak desk.

250

Ryo retrieved an antique magnifying glass from a side drawer and examined the crime scene photo. After several seconds of careful scrutiny, he handed the image back to her and pointed to the victim's left hand. "There; do you notice anything unusual?"

The woman frowned as she studied indicated spot, "Oh; one finger is missing!" She stared at him, "How does that figure into this, Ryo?"

"I'll let you know in a minute."

The old Investigator tapped away at his interface screen and scrolled through several grainy video clips before settled on one. "The time stamp is 10:32. This was taken at the Ballyshannon East Gate, although I'm afraid that the quality is not very good."

Helen craned her neck to study the video.

"OK, here we go," Ryo froze the video and slowly advanced through one frame at a time.

From high above the inspection area and a good five meters away, the border guard handed an interface device through the window of the vehicle to the delivery driver. The man swiped his left index finger over the screen and passed the device back to the guard before being waved through the gate.

Ryo toggled back and forth between several frames. He zoomed in on the driver's left hand. The image was especially grainy. "What do you notice about this?"

Helen bit her lip as she scrutinized the picture. "That's strange, he's got *six* fingers on his left hand."

"I'll bet a week's pay that he slid the dead man's digit over the interface screen, it's a gruesome old trick."

Ryo tapped out the delivery vehicle's ID number and a flashing red notation popped up: *Transport found abandon by Registry Bureau 3:28PM. Impounded at Ballaghaderreen District Lot. Unable to contact owner. Fine Due: 637 Standard Units.*

He summoned a Forensic Technician to the Impound Lot before looking up at the Cadet Inspector. "I've got a strange hunch about the creep who apparently murdered a delivery driver just to sneak into Free City. Let's dash over and take a look at the abandoned transport and see if we can find out who this guy is."

She nodded eagerly at the new assignment.

35. Slip-ups

"And the whole time that we were at the Fort of Djaba, we had no idea whether the Desert Serfs would shoot us or if we would manage to pull the operation off." Lev stopped abruptly and stared at Keira.

The woman had a ghastly look of horror after hearing the twin tales of Lev's rescue of Ryo and the Lieutenant in New Rome and the efforts to infect the Serfs with the strange pathogen.

"What is it, sweetie?" he stoked her cheek.

Her face slowly shifted from dread to resolve.

"I'm glad that you haven't been agitating in the streets of New Rome," she whispered in an uncharacteristically deep and rumbly tone, "but this spy work that you've been doing is really dangerous. I should know, Liaison Officers go through the same training as Intelligence personnel."

He laughed nervously at her unexpected response to his recent adventures, "I'm pretty tough."

"No;" she shook her head, "no, you're not. I worked with you and Ryo last year when we chased the pirates around the Solar System. It's a rough-and-tumble job that requires years of practice. You're not up to the rigors and riskiness of espionage and investigation. I see it all of the time in the Liaison Office, spies and cops live short and brutal lives."

He scolded at her harsh assessment.

"If we are going to marry," she glanced wishfully towards him, "and I certainly hope that we do, you need to settle on something that's safer."

"Like Ultra Energy Physics?"

Keira considered the tall, disheveled mop-top of a man that she had grown to love over the last year. He was *so* much more complicated than she had ever imagined. She had given up on trying to change him into a strait-laced Research Scientist months ago and recently had rather enjoyed him for who he really was: a restless and disorganized optimist. Any rigid dictate from her now would likely end their relationship and cast them both into a chasm of protracted misery.

"It's up to you," she finally replied.

• • •

They had been sequestered together in the tiny safe house for days.

"Are you excited about attending the parade tomorrow?" Sabra asked.

"Yes." Dilma pirouetted around and curtsied. Her face darkened and she added, "Also a little scared."

"About what?"

The girl smiled nervously, "Sabra, I'm afraid that I'll look silly in front of all of those people."

She was such a dear thing, the woman realized, much more innocent and wide-eyed about the world than other twelve-year-old girls.

"Sweetie, everyone will look silly."

Dilma thought about that assertion for several seconds. "Will it be OK to laugh at other people without hurting their feelings?"

Sabra grinned at the high-minded question, "It may hurt their feelings if you don't laugh."

• • •

Hours later Sabra awoke in the dark and quiet bedroom.

Some minor inconsistency was fluttering about in her head, but as of yet it hadn't solidified into a well-defined problem that she'd then be able to solve.

Dilma whimpered a bit as she slept in the other bed.

Her young charge seemed to be OK, Sabra realized, so that wasn't the problem.

The woman tussled for many minutes with the vague feeling that something had been overlooked as she fidgeted in the little bed.

Perhaps she should just get up.

She tiptoed into the hallway and glanced into Ryo's darkened bedroom. It was about 2 AM and her boss had not yet returned from work. Hopefully, for Dilma's sake, he'd join them for breakfast.

Sabra sat sleepily at the little dining table and studied the two costumes that took up a good portion of the surface. She and Dilma had spent much of their time during the unwanted isolation perfecting the finery for the parade.

She fingered the unusual fabric of her costume and it faintly glowed with the touch. It was made of a new luminescent material that responded to body heat that she'd found months ago at a specialty shop on Breton Street. The garment was sure to catch the eyes of many other parade participants.

Dilma's little getup was much simpler. The girl had painstakingly copied a whimsical drawing of an ocean denizen that she'd found and the results were remarkably true to the image.

Sabra gently spread the girl's outfit out on the table.

The woman realized that something was missing as she studied the garment.

The headband and the blue boa!

Dilma had asked Ryo to retrieve them from their apartment but the overworked Investigator had failed to do so. It was just a silly little thing, Sabra knew, but the girl would be especially unhappy if she did not have the items. Dilma might well hold Ryo accountable for his minor oversight.

That was the problem that had awakened her, Sabra realized.

But what to do about it?

She spent many minutes playing out various scenarios in her head to remedy the difficulty; all had significant shortcomings. Finally she concluded that she should sneak back to the apartment and pick up the missing items.

On the return trip she'd stop at her own abode
and retrieve a more appropriate pair of boots for
herself.

Surely a quick trip across town in the middle of
the night would be harmless.

• • •

The Forensic Technician glanced out of the cab
of the abandoned delivery vehicle when Ryo and
Cadet Inspector Helen MacDermish arrived at
the Impound Lot.

"Hey Ryo, what's got you up at this horrible
hour?"

The old Inspector waved to his longtime pal,
"Just catching up on some work. What have you
got?"

The Technician sighed, "Well; there's a dozen or
so small drops of blood on the floor, mainly right
around the driver's seat. I just ran some samples
through the Chromosomal Comparator and it
came back as Manfred Chong, age 37 from
Dublin."

Ryo nodded, "Mr. Chong *was* the driver
assigned to this vehicle."

He and Helen studied the cab's interior for several seconds.

Ryo rubbed his chin, "Manfred Chong was murdered nearly 24 hours ago. I suspect that you will find his DNA all over the cab. Check the steering wheel and perhaps the dashboard switches for fresh material from someone else."

"Already done." The Technician held up several swabs, "I just collected these, I'll run them through the Comparator right now.

While the machine was analyzing the specimens Ryo tapped out an update of the investigation for Helga when she returned to the office.

A pleasant ding from the Comparator announced the completion of the work.

The Technician read the results, "Herman Kowalski, age 28 from Nairobi. It says here that he goes by the name 'Bowie.' He has quite a record in EurAfrica. His current location is listed as unknown but I think that we can surmise that he's somewhere in Free City."

"The last of the Goons is now prowling around town," Ryo muttered.

Helen had a look of bewilderment, "Is that the criminal who murdered Manfred Chong?"

"It would be my guess but that particular investigation is in the hands of the Dublin Police." Ryo glowered in silence for a time, "I'm hunting for Herman 'Bowie' Kowalski for the murder of Mr. Nathan Briggs."

• • •

It was damp and dreary on the street.

For two long days Bowie had tried to locate Ryo Trop's kid and her nanny in Free City.

Fortunately he had some recent pictures and two pages of fairly good intelligence information to guide him.

Bowie studied a photo of the nanny. Her name was Sabra MacFarland and she was rather attractive. Too bad she was associated with Inspector Trop.

Apparently the old man had hidden them just after the dagger in the door incident. But no matter, Bowie thought as he leaned against the wall of a building on Rahara Street. He'd found out enough about the nanny to know that she shared an apartment with her sister about half a block down. All he had to do was to loiter around until she showed up and then trail her until she led him back to the hideout.

One way or another he'd murder the kid and the nanny and settle the score with Inspector Trop.

• • •

The old Landlady scrutinized the photo before she nodded.

"You're sure?" Ryo glanced at the gray-haired gal. She was in a grimy pink bathrobe with a headful of blue curlers. She hadn't objected too much when he knocked on the door of the boardinghouse at 3:30 AM. Apparently late night visits by the police were not uncommon.

"Yeah Inspector, that's him."

"You said he's not in at the moment;" Ryo continued, "any idea of where he is right now?"

"He doesn't seem to have a job," the Landlady frowned as she thought, "but he *did* ask a lot of questions about the Enlightenment Crusade and what those nut bags might be likely to do."

"What did you tell him?"

"Well; I've got a couple of Crusaders up on the third floor and all they talk about right now is the Bicentennial Parade tomorrow. He seemed really interested in that."

"Thank you. If he returns, contact me at once."

Torn From On High

She nodded sleepily before closing the door.

Ryo stood in grim silence for several seconds:
Dilma and Sabra would be at the parade.

• • •

Bowie was hunched over like a dozing vagrant,
but the big Goon certainly wasn't asleep.

About forty minutes earlier he'd spotted an
unusually wary young woman wrapped in a gray
cloak skulking down the deserted street. The
leery traveler nervously glanced around before
slipping into the apartment building that he'd
been watching.

Bowie then repositioned himself across the street
to afford a better view of the woman should she
reappear. He was fairly certain that it was Sabra
MacFarland.

The glass panes rattled in the ancient wooden
lobby doors of the apartment building.

Bowie glanced up.

The jittery woman stood in the dim early
morning light studying the empty thoroughfare
for far longer than would be considered normal.

It was her.

Bowie grinned malevolently before slumping forward to resume his ruse. He'd found the nanny.

She hurried off.

When she was nearly a block away, the big Goon stood and casually dusted himself off before following her.

Bowie patted the bulge in his jacket as he walked down the street; with luck he'd use the gun for killing today.

36. The parade

The swirling claptrap of the restless humanity
was deafening.

Sabra stood attired as a luminescent purple and
pink jellyfish in the midst of nearly thirty-five
thousand colorfully costumed parade
participants.

The huge group of revelers was stalled again for
some reason.

Dilma's quivery little hand was clamped tightly
to hers.

Sabra smiled at the tremulous twelve-year-old
who was elaborately dressed as a mermaid. The
girl was adorned with the hard-won headband
and blue boa.

Days earlier at the safe house Dilma had
managed to cajole Ryo into letting her attend the
huge public display that marked the end of the
Free City Bicentennial Exposition. Since
returning from New Rome, the old Investigator
had been strangely unwilling to let Dilma dawdle
about in the city.

The recent intimidation involving the dagger in
the apartment door had made her boss even more
edgy.

But Dilma's sparkling charm and endless persistence had eventually worn him down. Finally he relented with a few stern caveats: She must return to the safe house by sunset and must never be more than an arms length from Sabra during the entire outing.

The girl merrily agreed to his conditions before skipping off to work on her costume.

Sabra had noticed afterwards that Ryo watched over the girl as she fabricated her finery with an inexplicably moody look of foreboding.

But now it all seemed worth it, Dilma was participating in a once in a lifetime event that she certainly would relive for decades to come.

• • •

"OK; what is *that*?" Dilma pointed to the left at a group of a dozen or so parade participants in themed costumes.

Sabra studied the gang for several seconds before answering. "That's quite clever; it's a good portion of a chess set."

A man bedecked as a black rook shuffled forward and bumped a little girl who was dressed as a white pawn. The girl teetered dramatically before flopping to the ground. The move produced a booming call of "HUZZAH" from the other group members. The pieces reset themselves and the stylized sideshow began anew.

"Excuse me ladies," a deep male voice grunted.

Sabra turned to the new arrival.

"Jasper!" Dilma squealed with delight at the scruffy and imposing red-maned man dressed as a Neanderthal.

"G'day, sweetheart!"

Sabra scowled at the arrival of the unfamiliar man.

Dilma fingered the faux bearskin that wrapped the burly newcomer, "What are you doing here?"

He smiled at the young mermaid, "Ryo mentioned that you might need some company in the parade so I put on my Sunday best and decided to join you."

Sabra tipped her head in confusion, "How do you two know each other?"

"Ah...well...you see..," Dilma was uncharacteristically tongue-tied by the question.

The big man grinned pleasantly, "I helped her out of some difficulties about a year ago and eventually delivered her to Ryo."

"Yeah; that's it!" the girl quickly nodded in agreement.

Sabra frowned at the obviously over simplified explanation, up to this point everyone had been quite forthright in matters regarding the girl.

The parade lurched forward and the woman reluctantly set her leeriness aside.

• • •

Just to their right, an odd little Dixieland band was playing *When The Saints Go Marching In* with homemade scrap heap instruments.

The crowd had managed to move three blocks before the merry procession had stopped again.

It *was* especially festive, Sabra beamed.

After several minutes of awkwardness with the arrival of Jasper, Dilma had grasped his big hand and had shuffled proudly along between both of the adults.

The girl seemed quite comfortable with the big caveman, Sabra concluded.

WHACK!

Torn From On High

The sickening sound of bones cracking interrupted the high-spirited procession.

"HEY!" Jasper recoiled from punch. "WHAT THE..."

Dilma screamed.

Sabra turned to see a sneering thug in a black jacket, his hand still clenched up and bloody.

"BASTARD!" Jasper regained his footing and turned to the attacker. "I've got five years of bar brawls in Blackall," his fist slammed into the man's face, "and I've swatted bigger flies than you!"

The punk lurched back from the punch.

The crowd bolted away from the battling men.

Sabra instinctively jerked Dilma out of the way of the fracas.

"You're just in the wrong place at the wrong time!" the goon growled at Jasper. He produced an unusual gun and leveled it at the big Australian's head.

"NO!" Dilma lunged at the gunman just as he fired.

The punk was thrown off balance by the tiny

attacker.

A weird purplish beam crackled from the weapon and struck Jasper just above the right collarbone. A good-sized chunk of his shoulder blade was blasted away as the beam exited. Blood was everywhere. Jasper wobbled dizzily before he collapsed.

With spiteful satisfaction, the brute watched the big Aussie fall before he swung around towards Dilma, "NOW YOU!"

The twelve-year-old snarled defiantly as she slowly backed away from the man.

The assassin lined the gun up on the girl and pressed at the trigger.

In a blur of furious motion, the keen edge of a silver-gray broadsword struck the gunman across the small of the back.

"AHHH!" The bruiser winced in agony. His weapon clattered to the pavement.

The sword-wielder walloped him again behind the knees and produced a gaping wound. He crumpled to the ground.

The guardian angel pressed the razor-tipped broadsword between the thug's ribs should additional struggle require that he should be dispatched.

Three beat cops subdued the bloody man.

Several bystanders rushed in and tended to Jasper.

Dilma stared in awe of the small woman who had brought down the burly punk.

It was the mysterious redheaded woman that had prodded her to stay close to Sabra at the coffeehouse.

"IT'S YOU!" Sabra exclaimed as she studied their protector. "You loaned me money and introduced me to Ryo!"

"That's right, sweetie," she grinned enigmatically. "Someone named Zmuda had me keep an eye on you two from the beginning."

"Who's Zmuda?" Sabra wondered.

"Ah;" Dilma smiled, "he's my godfather!"

One of the cops withdrew a communications device from his belt, "We got him, Inspector Trop. We're over on Knutsford Street. Yes; it is definitely Bowie. Your kid and the nanny are fine but we need an ambulance for the assailant and a big chap named Jasper."

270

"Thank you," Sabra whispered to the mysterious woman.

The girl was still shaking from the violent altercation.

"I like this," Dilma nervously fingered the elaborate costume of their savor, "what are you?"

"I'm a Valkyrie. They're the death angels that carry slain Norse warriors away to Valhalla," she grinned at the wide-eyed kid, "or in this case, protect little girls from street punks."

The officer turned to the Valkyrie, "I'm going to need some personal details for the report."

She smiled curtly at the cop, "Edict 343 says you don't."

He nodded reluctantly and the redheaded death angel ambled off into the crowd with her bloodstained broadsword still in hand.

37. Jurisprudence

"How are you feeling, you big lug?" Mixion kissed his cheek.

"My shoulder's killing me," Jasper grimaced in the hospital bed, "I don't remember much after I got shot."

"Well the Lieutenant says you'll get combat pay, if that means anything."

She fiddled with the bed sheets, "They managed to rush you here and the Emergency Room Orthopedist took a bone sample. They're in the process of cloning a new scapula and clavicle that will be transplanted in place of the bones that were blasted away during the parade. Until they do the operation in two weeks you'll be hopped up on painkillers."

"Is Dilma OK?" The big man gnashed his teeth, "Did they get the guy with the gun?"

"She's fine; apparently the only reason that you weren't killed outright was that our little kitten shoved the attacker just as he fired. The CRAMP's new redheaded super-spy was trailing Dilma and her nanny. When all hell broke loose she did a fair job of neutralizing the situation."

Mixion's demeanor darkened, "Fortunately the

Goon is downstairs right now, locked up in the Prison Medical Ward."

• • •

"How's Jasper doing?" Zmuda wondered when he slipped into the CRAMP Situation Room.

Mixion produced a pleasant smile when you looked up from the monitor screen, "Well enough, considering what he's been through in the last few days."

The Lieutenant nodded, "That's certainly good news."

"I have another bit of luck to report." Mixion pointed at the latest satellite images from high above the ruins of the Fort of Djaba.

Zmuda studied the monitor.

The first high-resolution photo showed three men with orange and green headscarves apparently digging some sort of pit.

He tapped at the image, "Isn't that right around where the Serfs buried Daniel Kufuzu?"

Mixion nodded and switched to the second frame taken about ninety minutes later.

Two of the Desert Serfs were carrying a long

white shrouded bundle towards the pit.

"Mmm;" the Lieutenant stroked his chin, "I wonder if that's their most recent failed attempt to reclone Kufuzu?"

The final image showed the men filling in the pit.

Mixion snickered, "Well that would be number two if it is."

"Eventually they'll figure it out," Zmuda smiled.

• • •

"Alright Inspector Trop; you may begin," the stern Arraignment Judge stood over the shackled prisoner in the Medical Ward.

Two hefty guards watched over the proceedings.

"Thank you Justice Dwan."

Ryo turned and glared at the heavily bandaged Goon, "This man, Herman 'Bowie' Kowalski, has been charged with two counts of Murder in the First Degree for the killings for the purpose of intimidation of Debris Retrieval Specialist Third Class Nathan Briggs and Captain Philip Takahashi of the Low Earth Orbit Salvage Ship *Billikin*. Additionally he is charged with two counts of Assault with the intent to commit
274

murder upon Dilma Trop and Jasper Pomeroy on Knutsford Street in Free City."

Copiously restrained in his hospital bed, Bowie smirked as the old Inspector presented the charges.

The Judge turned to the cop, "What evidence do you intend to present at trial to support these allegations?"

"HE'S GOT NOTHING!" Bowie growled.

"Mr. Kowalski," the Judge snapped, "I will add one Contempt of Court Charge for each additional word that you utter during this formality."

The Goon stifled further comments.

"We've amassed quite a bit of evidence, Mr. Kowalski," the old Investigator glowered at the punk.

"You were found to be in possession of a unique weapon that has been traced by a preponderance of evidence directly to the murder of Nate Briggs. That weapon produced a very unusual tissue avulsion upon the body of Mr. Briggs which was nearly identical to a wound found on the remains of Captain Takahashi."

"That seems sufficient for arraignment but a

detailed presentation will be required at trial," the Judge interjected. "What of the evidence for the Assault charges, Inspector Trop?"

Ryo smiled with satisfaction at the question, "Since the crimes took place during the Bicentennial Parade, we have dozens of witnesses who will testify as to Mr. Kowalski's actions."

After several seconds of pondering the matter Judge Dwan spoke, "Let it be posted in the Official Daily Records of the Free City High Court that Herman "Bowie" Kowalski is to be held without bail and bound over for trail for the charges of murder and assault."

"Thank you, Your Honor."

• • •

"It's been a hell of a few weeks," Zmuda noted as he sat at the Conference Room table in the Inquisitor's Office.

"It certainly has," Helga wheezed.

She turned to Ryo, "Summarize the final details of your investigation into the misdeeds involving the *Billikin,* if you would Inspector."

Ryo shuffled through his paperwork, "On the 1st of August, a Retrieval Specialist from the
276

Billikin by the name of Nathan Briggs was murdered in Low Earth Orbit for the purpose of intimidation by a punk named Herman 'Bowie' Kowalski. I have very good evidence that Bowie and his gang called the Goons were hired by Frédéric Rameau who was the EurAfrican Commander of Covert Operations for the Northern District of Africa."

"Rameau also supplied the unusual weaponry," Zmuda interjected. "Sadly, the Commander died in a recent 'accident' at the Base."

"Remind me to stay on your good side!" Helga snorted.

Ryo continued, "Sometime later, the Goons boarded the *Billikin* and murdered the Captain and crew. Afterwards they were not shy about spreading the news of the slaughter around the fleet of Space Debris Salvage vessels. This, combined with several earlier acts of intimidation, greatly reduced the amount of scrap material that made its way into the Metals Market."

Helga's bushy eyebrows arched up, "And that caused the recent run-up on the Metals Commodity Market?"

The old Investigator nodded, "Fortunately the prices are now edging down with the resumption of normal salvage operations."

Helga tapped at her copy of the report, "There is no doubt in your mind that the Kufuzu family was the prime instigators of this manipulation?"

"None at all."

"Alright;" the weary Chief Investigator sighed, "I will forward that information to the Prime Minister and the High Court for further action. I'm afraid that the Kufuzus still retain a great deal of power in EurAfrica so nothing may come of this."

She turned to the Lieutenant; "I understand that you are currently accountable only to the Prime Minister, perhaps you would favor me with whatever information that you wish to share regarding your recent activities involving Daniel Kufuzu."

"Much of it is Top Secret, mainly due to the use of unusual personnel and tactics," Zmuda forewarned them, "but this is what I can tell you: Daniel Kufuzu, Former Warlord of EurAfrica is dead and will not return."

Both Ryo and Helga smiled approvingly at the news.

Zmuda continued, "Significant efforts by the Enlightenment Crusade in New Rome and Nairobi have brought about many reforms in the local governments and some slight improvements in the treatment of slaves and

278

Serfs. Elsewhere in EurAfrica I'm afraid that much work needs to be done to reduce corruption and to improve the lives of all."

The Lieutenant stopped short, "That's all that I can share right now."

"What of Edict 343?" Ryo wondered.

"It's still in full effect," Helga noted. "Anything else, gentlemen?"

Ryo turned to the Lieutenant, "Thanks for supplying the bodyguard for my kid."

"No problem; she is my beloved goddaughter after all. You're on you own for now. The particular spy that saved the day is off on another assignment."

"I suppose that her nanny and I can look after her." Ryo gathered up his paperwork, "Helga, I'd like to request a two week sabbatical."

The cranky old Chief Investigator for the Free City Inquisitor's Office scowled at the request, "Why do you need time off, Mr. Trop?"

Ryo slowly smiled, "Four women have rather sternly indicated that I need to attend a formal function in the Southern Hemisphere."

Helga sighed with visible annoyance, "Very well; but I expect you back in a fortnight."

38. Goodbye hello

The formalities would begin in two hours.

Considering how somber the event was supposed to be, Luis Hernandez could not stop smiling as he checked over the site.

It was a beautifully clear morning on South Georgia Island, the perfect type of day for a funeral.

As the sun slowly warmed the normally frozen soil in the cemetery of New Grytviken, he surveyed the two deep rectangular holes. The sides bore the recent tool marks from the arduous effort that had gone into chiseling the permafrost into suitable gravesites.

He had started the sad work in earnest two days after Seamus had died. Luis had first sent the Official Death Notification to the Free City Bureau of Records taking care to leave the location of death blank and listing the decedent's name as merely 'S. Nelson.' Keira Norton had contacted him three days later to confirm that the old man had died.

Both Luis and Keira had been teary-eyed by the end of the sad exchange.

Several hours later, he checked on the old man's

corpse. It had frozen solid on the porch of the little white cottage where he had left it. When Luis's sprained ankle had mended enough that he could walk again with some painful effort, he hobbled down to the harbor maintenance building and tinkered with the little electric service vehicle that had sat forlorn there for several years.

Fortunately, the antique lithium iron phosphate batteries readily accepted a fresh charge and the centuries old control system required only modest adjustments.

By midday, he was able to drive the plucky little cart up the bluff to the cottage. With great care he'd carried Seamus's body down the stairs and gently placed it on the back of the service vehicle.

As he inched away from the cottage with as much reverence as he could manage, Luis glanced back at the house that they had briefly shared.

There in the front window watching over the sad cortege was Moresby.

Luis then spent several hours preparing the old man's remains for a proper interment. He carefully dressed the stiff old man in the one and only suit that he had in his closet. Luis finished up by slipping the shiniest of the fat copper half pence coins from their poker game into his shirt pocket for good luck.

Luis methodically measured the body and drew out the plans for a simple casket. He hobbled around the derelict buildings of the harbor for several hours collecting suitable scraps of wood for the project. When he had enough acceptable material, the Harbor Master then labored for days to construct a coffin for the old man.

When the sad task was completed, he gently placed the body of his friend into the box.

Since then, Seamus had lain in state in the casket draped with a fine dark blue tablecloth centered on three sturdy sawhorses in the frigid harbor maintenance building.

Luis had planned to bury the old man in the springtime when the ground thawed and his ankle had properly mended.

Six days ago his gloomy plans had dramatically changed for the better.

Keira contacted him again with a carefully thought-out proposal and today was to be the culmination of the intended efforts.

Now, in the slowly warming morning air of New Grytviken, Luis slowly trailed his hand over the two caskets. One was the rustic homemade coffin that he'd lovingly constructed for Seamus and the other was the modest commercially produced box that contained Nate Briggs' body.

Both men would be laid to rest today in the cemetery that overlooked Cumberland East Bay.

Ryo and Keira had brought the remains of Nate Briggs back to South Georgia Island several days ago aboard an intercontinental aerial transport along with Ryo's adopted daughter Dilma, her nanny Sabra MacFarland and Ryo's sweetheart Dr. Jana Fesai. Jana's son Lev, who was also Keira's fiancé, had come along to help out.

But it was Sabra MacFarland who had caught his eye.

Keira, Lev, Luis and Sabra had taken turns digging the two gravesites in the frozen earth of the cemetery.

Luis had spent a few hours with each of them in turn teaching them how to use the jackhammer and bucket hoist that were needed to chip through the rock-hard soil. Keira and Lev were merely mediocre at the task but Sabra attacked it with admirable gusto.

He soon found that he was working with increasing regularity along side the gregarious and mud-stained young woman. Even little

Dilma had tagged along and helped out with the difficult work on several occasions.

During a short break yesterday while he, Sabra, and the girl were enjoying a snack in the midday sun, Luis studied the two and briefly imagined what it would be like if the woman stayed with him for good on South Georgia Island.

Sabra had noticed his protracted stare and had winked at him across the mound of dirt that separated them.

Last night they had taken a long walk around the harbor together and shared a demure kiss on the porch of the cottage.

This morning as the rest of the solemn group prepared for the funeral, he and Sabra had both sported pleasant grins.

• • •

"We are gathered here together," Ryo started, "to lay to rest these two weary souls."

Nearly everyone had bowed their heads in respect for the departed.

Ryo glanced sideways and noticed that Dilma was studying him with great interest as he spoke. The girl had never experienced a funeral before and Sabra had spent many hours beforehand describing the ritual in great detail to her.

"I never knew Nathan Briggs, but I understand that he was a good man and certainly a hard worker in his profession as a Space Debris Retrieval Specialist. Sadly; he met his end when he was torn from on high by the unforgiving hand of gravity and cast into the southern sea. Now, at last, he will find peace."

Luis and Keira nodded in agreement.

"But I did briefly know Seamus Franklin Nelson. He had a wonderfully salty perspective on life and was quite willing to sacrifice himself for the greater good of others. Both are admirable qualities in any man."

Ryo studied the others as he recounted his moments with Seamus.

Jana stood next to him with the supportive appearance of a very dear friend. Their rather sweet relationship seemed destined to slowly evolve into lifelong love. That pleasant prospect caused Ryo to grin for several seconds.

Standing across from him, Keira held hands with Lev and both had a profound look of sadness.

Ryo wondered for several minutes if their sorrow was due to the occasion or perhaps something else. Both had seemed rather cross with each other during the last few days.

Luis covered his eyes and whimpered. Sabra produced a tissue and handed it to the big man. She appeared to be quite concerned about his forlorn state. Luis finally dabbed his dark brown eyes. Of the seven mourners clustered around the two coffins, he was by far the most emotional.

And why shouldn't he be? Luis had lost his friend Seamus and had spent quite sometime laboring to discover Nate's identity in order to afford the dead man a proper burial.

In a day or two, Ryo realized, Luis would be alone again on South Georgia Island.

"...and so these two will return to Mother Earth from where we all have sprung." Ryo nodded to Dilma.

The girl approached the two caskets with the fine silk pouch that she had carried with her from Free City.

Dilma retrieved a handful of dried pale pink rose petals that she had collected for the funeral from the garden near the War Atrocities Monument in Roscommon Park.

Her voice cracked as she sprinkled the petals onto the caskets, "Although you are no longer
286

with us, you will *not* be forgotten."

Nearly everyone smiled at the girl's efforts, she had practiced it several times for them in the cottage.

One by one they filed slowly past the two coffins to pay their respects.

Keira laid her hand respectfully on Nate's coffin then erupted into a tremendous wail when she touched Seamus' casket.

Lev led her away.

Dilma clasped Jana's hand as they lingered for a time at the gravesites. Jana glanced at Ryo and the two exchanged a warm smile about the little girl's surprising show of affection towards the woman. The twelve-year old and middle-aged Research Scientist headed off together towards the cottage.

Ryo stood for many minutes in retrospection before he bowed to each of the boxes. Partway down the pathway, the old Inspector glanced back up towards graveyard and glimpsed Sabra and Luis standing alone together in the cemetery high above Cumberland East Bay.

The big man stood with slumped shoulders and Sabra had sidled up next to him and wrapped her arm around his waist. A single Storm-Petrel glided fluidly through the sapphire blue sky high above the couple.

Ryo studied the man and the woman nestled adoringly together on the bluff. They were obviously quite smitten with each other. The old Inspector smiled; Luis and Sabra seemed to be a perfect match for each other.

"It seems likely," Ryo chuckled as he turned back towards the cottage, "that I'll have to find a new nanny."

Appendix

Chief Inspector Helga Bennet of the Free City Inquisitor's Office Rumored to never sleep, the seventy-year-old Chief Inspector is well known and respected for her toughness and abilities to guide difficult investigations to successful conclusions.

Professor Malcolm Evans/ Lieutenant Zmuda As Head of the Department of Advanced Applied Molecular Biology at Free City University he is loved and admired by his students. Professor Evans is an occasional advisor for the Enlightenment Crusade. Little is known outside of the Prime Minister's Office about his alternative persona as Spy Master for the super secret CRAMP Operation.

Sabra MacFarland Nearly destitute and often characterized as idealistic and naive, Sabra attends Free City University as a part-time student in the Department of Experimental Studies. She frequently attends Enlightenment Crusade gatherings with her idolized older sister Desiree. Sabra yearns to make more of her life.

Edlin Classmate and minor friend of Sabra MacFarland at Free City University.

Sabina Finney Considered by many to be manipulative and dismissive, the mysterious redheaded CRAMP agent was recently cloned by Lieutenant Zmuda using the DNA of a long dead North American woman. Little else is known of this twenty-five year-old spy.

Tariq Head of the group of Paramilitarist Desert Serfs sent by Commander Frédéric Rameau to a secret hideout in the Sahara Desert just after the death of Daniel Kufuzu, the Exalted Warlord of EurAfrica.

The "mute" slave This tall, thin man is currently a General Facilities drudge at the sprawling EurAfrican Imperial Military Base in Tunis.

Commander of Covert Operations and Feudal Master of Paramilitarist Serfs Frédéric Rameau. Frédéric was personally appointed to the position of Head Spy for the Northern District of Africa when he thwarted a poorly planned coup six years ago. Daniel Kufuzu personally rewarded Frédéric with the prestigious appointment as thanks for preserving the Warlord's standing as the Supreme Leader of EurAfrica. Rameau's office is at the EurAfrican Imperial Military Base in Tunis.

Qadir A subordinate member of the Paramilitarist Desert Serfs.

Daniel Kufuzu, the Exalted Warlord of EurAfrica Supposedly killed by the massive explosion that destroyed the EurAfrican capital city of Arusha, rumors persist that the brutal Warlord somehow survived the disaster.

Mixion Fahmi This twenty-seven year-old Australian woman was cloned over a year ago by Lieutenant Zmuda at the CRAMP's secret lab in the basement of the Biology building at Free City University. Mixion has proved to be invaluable to the CRAMP's efforts to destabilize the regimes of the Warlords that dominate human affairs in the mid twenty-fifth century. Zmuda considers the perceptive young woman to be Second-in-Charge of the spy organization.

Jasper Pomeroy This husky redheaded CRAMP agent is nearly twenty-eight years old. Jasper is a recent clone of a rugged former farmhand from twenty-first century Blackall in Queensland, Australia. Unlike Mixion, he speaks with a noticeable accent.

Fiefdom Liaison Agent and Attack Craft Pilot Keira Norton Attractive and often sensitive, this twenty-seven year-old Free City resident is an especially talented up-and-coming Fiefdom Liaison Agent at the Department of External Affairs. The Registry Bureau recently certified Ms Norton as an Attack Craft Pilot. Keira has a rocky romantic relationship with Lev Fesai.

Seamus Franklin Nelson Seamus is a ninety-seven year-old former Engineer on the *Billikin* who currently resides in the quiet Eire District of Free City. For much of his life Mr. Nelson was a Serf in the Crewmen and Dockhands Federation. He was indentured for over fifty years to the owners and various Captains of the *Billikin*.

The Head of the Connaught School for Disadvantaged Girls Judgmental and persnickety, few outside of the acclaimed institution are fond of this dour old woman.

Luis Hernandez Caretaker of New Grytviken, Superintendent of South Georgia Island and Harbor Master of Cumberland East Bay.

Moresby Luis Hernandez's old gray tabby cat.

Herman "Bowie" Kowalski A washed out Paramilitarist, his strapping street punk is the brains behind the EurAfrican 'Goons Gang,'

Norman Rollo Rollo is a recent addition to the Goons Gang. He's considered by most people to be especially dim-witted.

Bertrum Hubert Schleim Also known as Schleim or Slime. A member of the Goons Gang.

Fritzi Reginald Wolfe Often called Wolf or Wolfie by others. Second-in command of the Goons Gang.

Fiefdom Liaison Agent Hugo Mackillroy Agent Mackillroy attends to matters for the Free City Department of External Affairs in New Rome and Nairobi. He is known by most in the Free City Inquisitor's Office as "Mac." Agent Mackillroy has served as a Liaison Agent for nearly thirty years. Mac is a longtime friend of Ryo Trop.

Lev Fesai An active and highly committed member of the idealistic Enlightenment Crusade, Lev is a faltering Grad student at Free City University's Department of Physics. Often quite a womanizer, Mr. Fesai has recently committed himself to a monogamous relationship with Keira Norton. The twenty-nine year-old is the only child of Dr. Jana Fesai Ph.D.

Inspector Second Class Zara Kamchatka Permanently stationed in Nairobi, Kamchatka tends to investigative matters in East Africa for the Free City Inquisitor's Office. Tough and wily, Inspector Kamchatka is often mentioned as a possible replacement for Helga Bennet as Chief Inspector.

Forensic Technician Second Class Nicola Jenks Nicola is a talented expert at uncovering hidden details of criminal activities. She is especially well known for her excellent efforts at signal and image enhancement.

Cadet Inspector Helen MacDermish This recent twenty-two-year-old addition to the Free City Inquisitor's Office works on routine investigative matters during the graveyard shift.

About the book

It was quite clear to me as I finished up work on the Science Fiction Action/Adventure novel *The Ripple in Space-Time* that the amusing and often horrific exploits of Inspector Ryo Trop, Lieutenant Zmuda, Jasper, Mixion and especially little Dilma should be continued. All three of my longtime editors also clamored for more tales from Free City and the moldering feudal fiefdoms beyond.

Shortly after *The Ripple in Space-Time* was published, I wrote *Dreg's Scamp* as the first chapter for a possible project with the irresistible title of *Torn From On High*. At the time, I was uncertain as to how Nate Briggs' most gruesome death would fit into a story or whether it would even include any of the characters from *The Ripple in Space-Time*. But the chapter and the book title just begged to be fleshed out into a story.

Unlike my previous six novels, I started *Torn From On High* without any idea as to how it would end. A month or so after beginning the project, I wrote Chapter 6 21.080N, 12.271E and the arc of the story came together in a long list of chapter summaries. The book was completed just after New Years Day in 2013.

The Ripple in Space-Time was mainly about the hard-boiled and Film Noir inspired detective Ryo Trop and the dreadful Post Apocalyptic world that followed a huge war sometime in our future. In *Torn From On High* I decided to develop many of the more interesting characters from *The Ripple in Space-Time* and give them a more terrestrial adventure. As a side note, some of the characters in the Free City Series will *also* appear in the very different MAC Series that is due out in a year or so; Hint: Think clones....

Several locations in *Torn From On High* were just as important as the characters. I decided that Nate's body would be discovered in a remote and bone-chilling location. For many years I have been a big fan of the Discovery Channel's *Deadliest Catch,* which is a rough and tumble series about the Bering Sea crab fishing industry. I briefly considered using Amaknak Island and the fishing port of Dutch Harbor in the Bering Sea. But I settled instead on the far-flung South Georgia Island and the long forgotten whaling port of Grytviken located half a world away in the South Atlantic.

I found the convoluted and little known history of Tunis, which has risen and fallen many times in its six thousand year history, equally fascinating. As the Barbary Coast pirates had done centuries ago, I made Tunis the center of skullduggery in the distant future of the Free City world.

I needed a particularly isolated site to tuck away the Desert Serfs as they tended to their secret project. Alternating between Google Earth images and Wikipedia entries, I selected the forsaken ruins of the Fort of Djaba in Niger. A thousand years ago the Fort protected an important trading route but, alas, the difficult environment and terrible isolation proved to be too much for those who were stationed there. To this day it is still nearly impossible to travel to the area. A few very rugged visitors have posted pictures and short videos from the site on line.

As *Torn From On High* is prepared for publication worldwide on the 2nd of May 2014, I have done some early work on book number three in the series. With luck, it too will be available soon. Updates and excerpts will be posted on my web site: www.sfchapman.com

Enjoy,

SF Chapman
Northern California, USA. March 2014.

From the files of the Free City Inquisitor's Office: ™
The Ripple in Space-Time

S F CHAPMAN

Book 1 of the *Free City* science fiction adventure series
***The Ripple in Space-Time* is available from Striped Cat**
Press at Amazon.com and fine booksellers worldwide.

Inspector Ryo Trop of the Free City Inquisitor's
Office is called in when the Lunar Ultra Energy Lab
is destroyed by a mysterious blast.

Ryo quickly discovers that a complex and sinister
scheme is afoot as he searches for clues in the
moldering feudal fiefdoms of the Warlords that
dominate human affairs in 2445.

As he struggles with the difficult case, the same
question keeps popping up: Could the recent wave of
space piracy be connected to the disaster?

A lifelong Northern Californian, S F Chapman traded his construction job for the more docile profession of novelist in 2008 when the US economy faltered.

The tireless author has since written eight books. His first, *I'm here to help* is a literary fiction novella about a teenage daughter looking for answers to some troubling inconsistencies in her birth certificate. *The Ripple in Space-Time* is Chapman's second book. It is an exciting science fiction detective adventure set in a moldering and corrupt future controlled by greedy warlords. The author's third novel *On the Back of the Beast* is an action-packed Contemporary Fiction tale about a massive earthquake that destroys the San Francisco Bay Area. Most recently Chapman has released a tantalizing sequel to *The Ripple in Space-Time* entitled *Torn From On High*.

Other completed works awaiting publication are the post-apocalyptic soft science fiction MAC Series consisting of *Floyd 5.136*, *Xea in the Library* and *Beyond the Habitable Limit*.

Chapman is currently finishing up a rough-and-tumble literary fiction novel about homelessness called *The Missive In The Margins*.

www.ingramcontent.com/pod-product-compliance
Lightning Source LLC
Chambersburg PA
CBHW070551260626
47161CB00002B/569